A Twisted Garden

Simon Quellen Field

A Twisted Garden

Cover art by Simon Quellen Field

A Kinetic MicroScience Book

Published by Kinetic MicroScience, LLC

19395 Montevina Road

Los Gatos, California, 95033

www.scitoys.com

First edition: November 2008

Second edition: February 2023

To Dan Even, "Abalone Dan" to those who know.

Chapter One

People irritate me.

Ask anyone who knows me. They'll say it's the other way around. That's OK with me. They're less irritating when they stay out of my way.

This state of affairs is due to my particular affliction, which was engineered before I was conceived, and over which I have no control. My affliction is why my face is ugly, why I have no friends, and why I am filthy rich, although not nearly as rich as everyone expected. What everyone expected is not what they got, but my particular problem is caused precisely by what everyone expected.

Don't expect. Whenever you try a difficult trick in front of a large audience, never say anything more than "Watch this". Then when something goes wrong, you can just say "See — that's the problem".

I'm what went wrong.

I don't hate people. I need people, just like anyone else. More than anyone else. They irritate me though.

On that particular night, I was driving around the city, looking for a particular type of woman. With my problem, I need to be particular. I need someone who needs me for something badly enough that they are willing to overlook my face and my equally ugly personality and lack of social skills. This usually means a broke alcoholic begging outside a liquor store. I provide what they need, and they provide what I need, and neither of us care that they hate me in the morning. Everyone hates me by then anyway. I irritate them.

My condition makes me hyper aware. I notice everything. I remember everything. I don't just mean that in a casual way, I'm not being loose with the language. I notice and remember everything

I see, hear, or smell, and I can recall memories all the way back to when I first opened my eyes. So, I know when people are lying to me, either by their blink rate, the pulse on their neck, the dilation of their eyes, or simply by remembering every detail of everything they have ever said to me. You might not think that would be irritating, but you'd be wrong. It bugs the shit out of me. And when I point out the lies, or some other flaw or inadequacy, they get irritated. A well socialized person would not mention these things. But the more irritated I get, the less likely I am to be well socialized.

There aren't a lot of penniless drunk women standing outside liquor stores at three in the morning. I'd been cruising since before midnight, and the car was indicating it needed to be plugged in soon. I had more than enough charge to get home, but not enough for another hour of creeping around the low rent district.

There were two young women outside Lawrence Liquors on Third. The type I needed never came in pairs, but my brain was on autopilot, and my subconscious told me to stop here. Sometimes I can piece together how my brain comes to these decisions, but as often as not, the pattern it recognizes is below the conscious level, or composed of too many variables for the higher levels of the brain to accommodate. I drove around the block and parked.

It never helps to let them see the car. The less information they have, the fewer conclusions they draw. Come to them a blank, and you have more control of the situation. I walked around the block, approaching them from the direction they were facing, so they had plenty of time to get used to the idea that someone was coming in their direction. The sensible, sensitive types will move. The needy ones will stay. These two stayed.

The taller of the two had blonde hair in need of a hairbrush, but she was strikingly good looking nonetheless. She had a lean and slightly muscular, athletic figure. Her clothing was in the current style, but looked like she had slept in it more than one night. The other one was hurting. She had brown hair, equally hand-combed, and her eyes had the wetness of near tears, or old tears, and she shifted from one foot to the other, looking anxious.

The taller one stepped forward as I approached. I stopped and watched her as she studied me carefully. Neither of us spoke. Then she made her decision, and turned so I could see her friend behind her.

"Becca's cribbing bad on T," she said. "She needs a party, are you up to hosting?"

I started to answer, but the part of my brain that constantly analyzed things in the background was screaming to wait, something was wrong. Her accent was not local, and the mix of street slang and plain language was wrong. What sounded at first like clear English was in fact a code for something I was not familiar with. Time to get more information.

"She's coming down off something, I didn't catch what."

"T. Trip," she said, looking for recognition in my eyes. "Are you a party? She needs a host, bad. She's really good when she's on, you won't regret the shift, I promise."

The brunette nodded, looking at me anxiously. I made my own decision.

"I'd like to help. What is it you need from me?"

The blonde looked puzzled and apprehensive for a moment. "She has her own stuff. Just be kind to her for the next eight hours, enjoy the ride. But I stay with her. Maybe in the next room, but never far. Deal?"

I nodded. "I can do that."

The brunette finally spoke. "Oh, thank god!" she said, and pulled a small case from her pocket, and removed a tiny white object. She stepped over to stand uncomfortably close to me, and put one hand on my shoulder as the other brought the tiny pill to her tongue. She held my gaze closely as the pill dissolved in her mouth. She took a deep breath, and brought the other hand up to the back of my neck, and gently caressed my hair. She let the breath out slowly, and sank against my chest, her arms wrapping around my back. "Thank you so much," she said.

I had no idea what was going on. But the warm feel of her breasts on my chest, and the secure but gentle hug of her arms felt like what I had come here for. I looked over at the blonde, who still looked protective and doubtful, and saw movement out of corner of my eye as someone entered the liquor store. Something wasn't right.

I stood a little taller and looked around. There were five cars in sight. One was parked at a slight angle to the curb, the door not quite closed. It had no front license plate. I moved slightly to my left to get a better glimpse into the store, and I could see the face of the clerk at the register, but nothing more of the person who had entered.

"Do you have a phone I could use for a moment?" I asked the blonde. She hesitated a moment, then pulled one from the front pocket of her jeans. I opened it up, and dialed 911. The robot voice answered immediately.

"I'd like to report an armed robbery in progress, on the corner of Third and Lawrence, Lawrence Liquors. Caucasian man, six foot four and a half inches, wearing a knee length brown fake leather coat, last year's Nike's, and a Yankees baseball cap. He's driving a blue two-door Cria with no front plate, tires with maybe a thousand miles left on them, dent in the left rear fender. It's a 2072 model, so it won't have a charge for more than 30 miles, so he'll be looking to plug it in or abandon it. He's left-handed, and has a pointed nose, no facial piercings or tattoos, and no facial hair."

I moved the women out of the light and closed the phone.

"I'll buy you another one as soon as we get out of here," I said, and threw the phone onto the roof. The blonde began to look indignant but a loud shotgun blast from inside the store caused her to close her mouth and move farther into the shadows. *Make that a robbery homicide*, I thought to myself.

The man in the long coat ran from the store with a paper bag, opened the car door and slid inside quickly. The electric motors whined as he sped away, weaving a little as the driver settled into the seat.

The blonde moved towards the door of the liquor store, and I caught the sleeve of her blouse.

"Wrong direction," I said, and steered the two back along the street the way I had come.

"Someone could be hurt in there," she said.

"Someone is dead in there. There's nothing you can do but get locked up for possession."

"Who was that guy? You knew everything about him."

"Never saw him before."

"How did you know he was robbing the store?"

We turned the corner. I could hear sirens already. "On a hot night like this, who would be wearing a long jacket? Someone hiding a shotgun. Who hides a shotgun when they go into a liquor store? Who parks in a hurry and leaves the door half open? Who ignores a stunning blonde under a street light and only sees the door to the store?"

"You only glanced at him. How did you know all that about him, like exactly how tall he was?"

We turned the second corner, and I could see my car.

"He stood up in the doorway as he checked for customers. A standard doorway is 80 inches. He cleared it by three. Add half an inch for the cap."

She took this in as the car recognized my voice and lit the interior lights. She noticed it was a two-seater.

"You two take shotgun," she said. "I'll drive, unless you live out of town."

I nodded, and the two of us got in, and the brunette slid onto my lap, wiggling perhaps a little more than necessary. She seemed very happy, and quite oblivious to all that was going on.

The blonde shut her door, and said "Home," to the car. The car ignored her.

"Parkside," I said, and the car began to move. The blonde looked over at me.

"OK, I guess you're driving."

The car picked up speed on the empty street. The brunette nuzzled my ear and giggled. "You threw her phone on the roof." She seemed to think this was quite amusing.

"The dispatcher has a lock on the phone, they could have tracked us wherever we went." I looked over at the blonde. "You had no numbers stored, and 17 minutes of time left, so I knew it was a disposable. They won't know who owned it until they swab it for DNA.

By then they'll know who phoned in the tip, anyway, so it won't matter."

"I'm not in any database. No record," she said.

"I am. I'm in all of them," I said. "But it won't matter — they won't know until sometime tomorrow, and by then your friend won't set off sniffer alarms at the station."

She was silent, taking in all that had happened in the last half hour.

"So, what is T?" I asked.

The look she gave me punctuated the anger in her voice. "You promised eight hours. After that, we're out of your hair. But if you back out now, I swear I'll rip your lungs out with my bare hands."

"Eight hours. More if you need it. I promise. But what is she on?"

"I don't know what you call it on this coast. We call it Trip, or T. They used to call them love beads in England."

"Tryptamino JDL synthase?"

"I think so. You know it?"

"Not enough to know what to expect. Hits the dopamine, oxytocin, and serotonin pathways, highly addictive, mood altering. But there are dozens of variants. How does this one present?"

"Are you a doctor?" she asked.

I thought about how to answer that. "I have the degree, but I don't practice."

"Here's what you signed up for. She's imprinted on you. For the next seven and a half hours, you are her whole world. She'll do anything for you. She loves you like puppies and ice cream. Most guys take advantage, so that's why I'm here, to keep her away from guys who want to hurt her, or trick her out for money. So have your jollies tonight, she'll make you really happy, but if you hurt her, you're a dead man, you hear me?"

The brunette had heard this lecture before, and giggled as she squirmed in my lap. I considered what I had just heard. "She's safe with me. You can watch us all night."

She wrinkled her face. "You'd probably like that. I'll stay in another room, thank you. And she'll hate your guts in the morning."

"I'm used to that."

"No, I mean really hate your guts. It's a reaction to the drug. Don't keep anything sharp around when she comes out of it."

The car slowed and waited for the gate to fully open, then drove into my driveway. We drove through the grove of oaks, then turned to park in front of the marble columns at the front entrance. The car is programmed to use the front when there is a passenger with me — perhaps I should have overridden that.

"You live here?" the blonde asked.

"Most of the year," I said as Becca slid off my lap with a giggle and turned to help me out of the car. I don't need help, but she seemed to like bending over in front of me.

"My name's Jack," I said to the blonde as I gestured to the porch stairs.

"Cat," she said, taking the stairs three at a time.

I introduced them to the door. "Becca and Cat, full access, all privileges, guest credit. No time limit, no video indoors."

"Welcome Becca, welcome Cat," the door said, and opened both doors wide.

The front parlor is designed to impress and intimidate. The size of a basketball court, framed by two sweeping wide curved staircases, it looks like something out of *Gone with The Wind*, but on a bigger budget. I prefer the back entrance.

"Where's the butler?" Cat said, gently mocking, but probably expecting one to show up any time.

"I live alone," I said, walking through the large room towards the hallway opposite the door. The doors closed behind us. Becca finally stopped staring at me and noticed her surroundings, eyes wide, but kept hold of my hand as we entered the hall.

"Are you hungry, would you like something to drink?" I said as we got to the kitchen. I waved at the refrigerators and the bar, but Cat shook her head.

"Where's the bathroom?" she asked. A painting on the wall of the hallway became a map of the house.

"Feel free to explore around," I said. "Nothing's off limits or private."

"I want to see your bedroom," Becca said, nuzzling up against my shoulder.

"That's upstairs," I said, pointing to the map. "Cat can have any of these rooms. We'll leave the door open so you can call to her any time you like."

Cat gave me a look, then went to find the bathroom. Becca and I went upstairs.

My bedroom is the size of the house I was born in. It's mostly windows, looking out into the oak grove and the gardens. The bed is in the middle, and around the edges are couches, overstuffed chairs, and a large desk with monitors where I work. Becca found

the master bath, then went in while I checked for new correspondence at the desk. There was a long list, but nothing that had to be
attended to at four in the morning. Especially the flashing message
from the police department.

I had just cleared the monitor when Becca came out of the bathroom, wearing nothing. She had found a hairbrush, and had
washed her face. She walked slowly to the bed, and poured herself
onto it, without pulling back the covers. She rested her head on
one hand, her elbow sinking into the bed, and grinned at my ap-
praisal.

I walked to the bed and sat down next to her. She pulled me down
and kissed me, wrapping her arms tightly behind my back. I slid
down next to her and put my arm under her head and my other
hand on her shoulder. She pulled that one down to her breast.

I felt protective — she was so vulnerable. I was highly aroused, but
taking the obvious next step seemed very wrong. I removed my
hand from her breast slowly, and stroked her hair, her shoulders,
ending at the cradle of her waist just under the rib cage. She smiled
and stretched, and began unbuttoning my shirt. I kicked off my
shoes, and removed my pants, leaving my underwear on. I had a
feeling that if I didn't, there would be no way I could resist taking
advantage of the drug's effects on Becca. And while parts of me
were more than ready to do just that, the part of me that makes my
other decisions was not comfortable with the idea.

I pulled back the covers and we both slid under them. I cradled her
head on my arm again, and kissed her on the forehead.

"I think this is what I needed," I lied, "just some warm cuddling and
company."

"You know you can have anything you want — things no other
woman will do for you, or let you do." She moved over on top of
me, pressing against my erection, moving her hips slowly.

"Is there something you need from *me*?" I asked. I wanted to do something for her, make her happy. If she needed sex, I would give her sex.

"I just want to make you happy," she said, smiling.

"I'm very happy just having you here next to me. Aren't you the least bit sleepy? I know I am."

"I won't be able to sleep until it wears off. Am I keeping you awake? Do you want me to be quiet?" She moved off me, but kept maximum skin contact as she settled by my side.

I just smiled and kissed her forehead, then laid my head on the pillow and closed my eyes.

She whispered "lights off", and the room faded to dark. I pretended to sleep, feeling her warm breath on my ear, feeling her breast against my side move as she breathed. It was a long time before I stopped pretending and actually slept.

It was well after noon the next day when I woke up. Becca had rolled over to her side of the bed, and was sleeping quietly. I slipped out of the bed slowly, trying not to wake her, and picked up my clothes and left the room without a sound. The windows were still dark, but the open doorway was dimly lit from light coming from under the door of the room opposite. Cat must have picked that room.

I carried my clothes down to the gym on the first floor, and pulled a clean pair of shorts out of the closet by the shower. The gym has a lot of equipment I no longer use, but nicely fills up the large room. My workout starts with a run uphill on the treadmill, then the weight machines, then walking the rack of dumbbells from large to small until I can't lift the lightest one. I was just starting on the rack when I heard shouting upstairs. I put down the weights and listened.

The house has pretty good soundproofing, so I could only make out the words that were shouted loudest. Mostly these were words like "asshole", "fucker", and the like, but occasionally I could make out whole sentences, like "What am I, not even good enough to fuck? Who does he think he is?"

Becca was awake, and she was not happy. She was also quite a bit more communicative than she had been the night before. I went back to the weights, replaying what Cat had told me about Becca hating me in the morning. If we had had sex, would she have been as upset at that as she was at its absence?

The shouting upstairs stopped, and I thought I could hear the shower running. I had worked my way to the middle of the dumb-bell rack when Cat cleared her throat in the doorway.

"Quite a sweat you've worked up," she said, walking from machine to machine, examining everything. I set down the weights.

"How's Becca?"

"She's pissed. That's normal. She'll flip between bawling and shouting for an hour or two, then she'll crash again. She'd love to shout in your face, but if she starts crying, pretend you don't notice. She hates it when people see her cry. We'll be out of your hair real soon."

"Stay as long as you like. There's plenty of room here. No need to sleep out in the open again tonight."

She looked at me closely. "She's not going to go back to being your love slave you know."

"I hope not. I'm much more comfortable with people hating my guts. I'm used to that."

"You keep saying shit like that," she said. She stepped up to the treadmill and pressed the resume button. The machine rose up to a steep grade and began moving swiftly. She was surprised, but managed to keep the pace. I was impressed. She pressed another button and the wall screen in front of the treadmill presented a jog-ging path through the woods, and a figure jogging on the path ahead of her.

She looked down at the controls. "You did half an hour of this?"

"The machine varies the workout," I said. I didn't mention that she was on the easier part of the circuit.

She kept the pace comfortably, not breathing hard yet. I was more impressed. I went back to the rack of dumbbells, and picked up where I had left off.

She was still at it when I finished the rack, and I went into the shower. The shower is just a large room with four shower heads and no door. I could hear her feet on the treadmill as I took off my shorts and started the water. I did not hear them stop since I had my head under the shower. I was washing my hair when she came in and stood watching me. I rinsed the shampoo from my hair and returned her gaze. I felt glad that my first reaction was not to cover my nakedness and gasp.

"You gay?" she asked, removing her shoes.

"I don't think so," I replied. I reached for the soap. She removed her shirt, then her bra, and then removed her pants with a grace and balance I doubted I could replicate. She slipped out of her underwear and walked to the showerhead next to mine.

"Why didn't you fuck her?"

"It didn't seem to be what she needed."

"What the hell do you care?" she asked, turning on the water and stepping under the showerhead.

I thought about my reply. "I think I'm used to women who are a little more mercenary in that department. Quid pro quo."

"She got what she needed. You missed out. Your quid got no quo."

"She was very nice," I said.

"She was head over heels for you, you dipshit. She would have been much more than nice if you'd let her."

"Is that what has upset her?" I asked.

"Fuck no. She doesn't give a shit. She hates you as much as she hates the guy who had his friends ass rape her for eight hours. Once she comes down, you're all assholes. It's how the stuff works."

"Someone did that to her?"

"Before I started coming along. She was in the hospital for a week, until she started cribbing again and I helped her spring out. I told the next party nothing more than blowjobs or I'd castrate him."

I looked down at her well-defined arms and trimly muscular legs and didn't doubt that she was capable. She noticed my glance and slowly turned around under the spray, letting me see the whole effect. She looked down for my reaction and asked "You sure you're not gay?"

I smiled and turned off the water. She did the same, and we grabbed towels and dried off. I handed her a terry robe from the closet and she scooped up her clothes.

"Leave those for the housekeeper, she comes later today, she'll get them washed and folded for you. In the meantime, order what you want and the house will have them delivered."

"Is that what 'guest credit' means? I can order shit on the net and the house pays for it?"

"Up to a certain limit, yes."

"Cool. I'll max it out."

I smiled, and we walked through the house to the kitchen, where Becca was already sitting at the bar eating cold cereal. "Keep your distance, asshole," she said. "And why the hell don't you fix that ugly face? All this money and you can't afford a little plastic surgery? My dog wouldn't wear that face in public."

"Good morning," I said, walking to the refrigerator. "Would you two like to share an omelet with me?"

"Fuck off," Becca said, and left the kitchen, stomping heavily up the stairs to the bedroom.

"Got any meat?" Cat asked.

I put the eggs back in the refrigerator and pulled out a couple of steaks. "Can I leave these with you while I make a phone call?" I asked. She nodded, and I went into the downstairs media center.

The message from the police station was still flashing. I tapped it with my finger, and the wall showed a busy police station behind a large familiar face.

"Cute trick, asshole," the face said congenially. "You know every-one in the station knew who placed the call the moment they heard the description. Get your butt down here and fill out the paper."

There was a follow-up message after that one. I tapped the screen again, and the same face reappeared, this time looking much more concerned. "You're a material witness to two homicides now. Get your butt down here. The guy in the long coat blew the face off the liquor store clerk, and then we found his ass dead in his car, some sort of nerve agent all over his face. Two uniforms are in the hos-pital after touching it. If you're not down here by 5 o'clock, I'm sending a SWAT team over there with a warrant."

I looked at the time. Plenty of time for a nice breakfast. Or lunch — it was much too late for breakfast.

In the kitchen, Cat was sawing at a dry brick of something that used to be a prime steak. I picked up the brick on the plate that must have been meant for me and walked over to the trash compactor. "You don't microwave a steak," I said.

I got two more out of the refrigerator, and opened the broiler. "Six minutes on a side," I said, and placed them on the rack and closed the door.

"I never cooked anything except in a microwave," Cat said, less con-trite than defiant. I pulled out a bowl and started slicing fresh peaches and strawberries into it for a fruit salad, then poured two glasses of orange juice. The broiler tinged, and I turned the steaks. The aroma began to fill the kitchen.

Cat was halfway done with her brick, stubbornly continuing to eat when I placed the juicy steaming replacement on her plate. She cut off a bite and chewed. "Thought that first one was a little dry and tough," she said.

We ate. She said nothing, but appeared to savor the simple meal.

"I have to go out and take care of some things. A few hours. It's best if you two stay in, out of sight for a while — the police are probably watching the street. They don't know about the two of you yet, and it looks unlikely that they'll try to find your phone. They know who phoned the report in. I'll be down at the station being interviewed."

"You want us to stay here alone?"

"It's not the worst place in the world to spend a few hours. Watch a movie, shop on the net, get some new clothes and a new phone. Take a swim."

"You trust us?"

"Aren't you trustworthy?" I asked.

"We won't fuck anything up."

"Most things are easily repaired. They're just things. Have fun."

I got up to leave. "Oh, the housekeeper will be here soon. Don't frighten her. I'm never here when she's working, so she's used to having the place to herself."

"We'll stay out of the way."

The car had parked itself in the garage after dropping us at the front door, so I walked to the back of the house and out the big double doors. I looked over the cars available, and chose the big black sedan. Arriving at the station in a limousine was exactly the right touch. People in limos get less shit from people on government salaries.

Once I entered the station itself, however, none of that mattered. Everyone here knew me.

"Hi asshole," said the desk clerk. "He's at his desk." She buzzed me in, and I walked past a row of desks, some empty, some with faces that recognized me and then went back to work.

"About fucking time," a voice called out. Sammy stood up from his desk and came to meet me.

He held a printout of a man slumped in his car, eyes open, a slight redness across the skin.

"This your guy?" he asked. I glanced at the paper in his hand.

"That's the guy. Missing the hat, but that's him."

"The guy that took his hat off to take the picture is in the hospital. Some kind of crap was sprayed on the hat and this guy's face. The guy's on a respirator while they flush his system."

I waited. Sammy looked up at me.

"So, what were you doing downtown at three in the morning?"

"Going to a liquor store," I said.

"You don't drink, asshole."

"Is this material?" I asked.

"How the fuck should I know? Damn clerk got his face blown off, nothing missing from the till, no witnesses but you. Who'd hit a night clerk and not take the money? Did something scare the guy off? Did the gun go off accidentally, and the guy panicked? Who killed the shooter, and how come? All I got is you, genius. Spill."

"He left with a paper bag. Did you find that in the car?"

"Hey Jimmy, was there a paper bag at the scene?" Sammy called out.

"No bags, car was stripped. Just the dead dude."

"It was no accident. The pump action was racked just before the shot."

"You knew it was a shooting and you didn't report it?" Sammy asked, with exasperation.

"I could hear the sirens. I had other places I needed to be right then."

"I'll bet you did. This just stinks. What was in the bag?"

"Not much. Perhaps a pound or less of something, not bulky. The bag had been carried before, the wrinkles at the top weren't new."

"How you do that is just spooky. You saw the guy for what, ten seconds max."

"You know me, Sammy. You know how it works."

"Just spooky. So, small bag, like a lunch bag or something? Maybe had a sandwich in it?"

"Or designer drugs. Something worth killing for, but small. Normal street drugs in small quantities wouldn't attract the kind of people who have access to nerve agents. If it were information, it would be sent electronically, or pocketed, not put in a brown paper bag at a liquor store."

"What kind of designer drugs are we looking for?"

"Ever heard of Tryptamino JDL synthase?" I asked. "Highly addictive, made its way from Europe to the east coast, and last night I learned it's here in the city."

"You learned this last night."

"Yes."

"Outside a liquor store."

"Yes."

"Shit. Fuck you. I'm sitting here on a double homicide, with cops in the hospital, and my brother is sitting on critical information he got while right in the middle of all the shit going down. You know why everyone who's known you more than five minutes calls you asshole? It's shit like that."

I shrugged. We both knew it was more than that.

I spent the next two hours dictating everything I had seen and remembered into the station computer. I left out certain details pertaining to my new acquaintances, but there was still a lot of detail to record. Having a perfect memory really is a curse.

§

Chapter Two

Cat and Becca were in the downstairs media room when I got home. Becca spoke first.

"Hey pervert. At least we figured out the faggot thing."

I had missed something. I'm not used to that. I cocked my head and waited for more information.

"We met your housekeeper," Cat offered.

"Did she get your laundry done?" I asked, noting that Cat was still in the robe from the shower.

The women found this highly amusing.

Becca said "We heard some noise and came down, and there she was, buck naked pushing a vacuum cleaner. She seemed surprised to have a live audience."

"She puts on quite a show for the cameras," Cat said.

"The cameras are always off when she's here," I said. "The house knows who should be here and who shouldn't, and never monitors people who belong here."

Cat wasn't having any of it. "You hire a hooker to clean your house naked, and you're never there to watch, and you don't record the show. Right."

"She's not a prostitute, she's a housekeeper," I said, no longer convinced myself.

"She washes the fucking windows with her tits!" Becca almost shouted, quite pleased with herself.

"She says she gets six grand a week for full service, but has never had to put out yet," Cat said. "You have a problem with intimacy going on here? I sense a pattern."

"She advertised as a housekeeper. After the first four housekeepers quit, I figured the high price was because word had gotten out. And yes, she offered full service for another couple thousand, so I figured I'd get the best service. But I always make sure I'm out of the house when she's here — it's too hard finding someone to do the work."

Cat was sliding off the sofa covering her face and laughing. "I can just see the advertisement. Full of double entendres so she doesn't get busted right out, and you paying top dollar for 'full service' thinking it's going to mean she takes out the garbage."

Becca chimed in. "You really ought to record the show. She works her butt off flashing the cameras and doing aerobic dusting, it's really a shame that all that goes to waste."

I was somewhat amused myself. "She really does do a good job on the windows," I said lamely.

Cat gracefully changed the subject before Becca could work up vitriol. "How did it go with the cops?"

"The guy with the shotgun was found dead in his car a few miles away. Someone had relieved him of the paper bag he ran out of the store with. The detectives wanted to know what was in the bag that was worth two murders."

"They thought you would know what was in the bag?" Cat asked.

"One of the detectives is my brother. So, yes, he thought I would know. I made up some bullshit about designer drugs and told him I'd heard that JDL synthases had made it to this coast and that seemed to make him happy. Makes no sense though."

"Nothing you say makes any sense," Becca said.

"You carry yours in your pocket," I explained. "You could carry ten thousand doses in your pocket. No one would use a liquor store as a drop for something they could just as easily carry around in their pocket. No, the liquor store makes sense if the bag held biologicals. The store is full of refrigerators and freezer compartments. And the right biological can be worth murder to some people."

Cat said "So, your brother is a cop, and you lied to the cops about a murder case, just for the fun of it. And you jump to wild conclusions based on next to nothing. Or are you leaving something out?"

"The assailant was killed by a nerve agent sprayed in his face. Not a lot of people have access to that kind of murder weapon. But someone stealing high-end biologicals would not find it that hard to acquire or manufacture."

The women were spared the rest of my lecture when the house chimed softly.

"Ah, duty calls. Got to get to work," I said, and left the room.

The upstairs media room is where most of my work is done. Unlike the downstairs version, which has couches and comfortable chairs facing the screens and a snack bar, the upstairs room is Spartan, and dedicated to a curving wall of large monitors filled with color coded graphs. There are no chairs — I work standing up.

The cause of the interruption was flashing on one of the screens. I touched it and the monitor on the left changed to a tangled display of graphed lines in various colors. Out of the corner of my eye I saw Cat enter the room.

"You said we could explore. Is it OK to watch?"

"Sure. Not a lot to see." I pointed to the flashing line of text. "That's a trigger. I tell the system what to watch for, and when that thing comes up, I get notified."

She scanned the huge screens, full of tables, charts, and colored lines. "Start at the beginning. What am I looking at here?"

"Economic data. I look for patterns. Some patterns hint at things like insider trading, or indicate what a highly placed executive really thinks about his company, or how a new engineered crop is going to handle the weather over the next 6 months. If I see a pattern, I set a trigger. The trigger fires when something in the pattern repeats, indicating a confirmation. Sometimes I buy or sell a stock or an option based on the information, but I can usually make a lot more money selling the pattern to a hedge fund."

"So, what's the pattern here?"

I pointed at a red line on a graph, then at a blue bar on the other monitor, then at a table below that. Then I swept my hand across the monitor on the left, with its tangle of fine colored lines. "People are buying freezers. There's a profit surge in three large warehouse food chains that sell food in bulk. The cost of air travel has gone up. And Vitally Orbison has come out with a new fashion line, featuring short skirts. These here," I said, waving at the tangled lines, "have a general trend indicating that people are putting off buying large appliances and automobiles."

"So, where's the pattern?"

"Vitally Orbison is not going to sell a lot of short skirts. That in itself is not valuable knowledge. But here is the trigger. This small company has leveraged itself to provide VO with the fabrics for those skirts. When they don't sell, these guys will be in the kind of trouble they can't escape. Potential buyers are these three firms, and these two will pick up the business from VO. It's time to place two puts, here, and here, and a call here. About eight percent of variability on each of the puts, and twelve percent of variability on the call."

The house spoke. "You have placed a spending limit of twenty-two million on the Barclay's account. Do you wish to override?"

"How much are we over?" I asked.

"Seven point three one percent," came the answer.

"Override. Move that amount from British long bonds into Barclay's and reset the limit to eighteen million once the transactions clear."

Cat was still staring at the screens. "How do you see all that in this mess?"

"I don't. This is just today's data, on what I told the system to watch on Monday. A drop in the bucket. My skill is in not forgetting any of it, and letting my subconscious run correlations on it all while I sleep or pick up loose women outside liquor stores."

Cat kept looking at the screens. The moment of silence stretched, and I could see her breathing slow as she stood in thought.

"Your guests have a budget to spend on clothes and shit?" she said, finally.

"Yes," I replied.

"House," she said into the air, "put my budget on the same things he just bought. And sell it when he does." She looked over at me. "I don't need clothes."

Several smart remarks crossed my mind, but I kept my silence.

Becca shouted from downstairs. "Hey asshole, what did you tell the police about us?"

Cat and I went downstairs. In the media room, Becca was watching a news station. She looked at me angrily. "They're talking about the two dead guys. They say they're looking for a witness, some chick hanging around the liquor store."

My brother can put two and two together. Unknown female DNA on the disposable phone tossed onto the roof.

Cat picked up on it right away. "They found my phone."

"And they let the whole world know there was a witness to a drug gang murder. All the cameras we passed by. They'll be giving our photographs out on the nightly news. Then someone can come and pop us off too. Just great." Becca was livid.

"You can stay here until this blows over," I said.

"Oh, that's just great! Locked up with the pervert for who knows how long? What about when I need another party? I order him on the net? This is just fucked."

I closed my eyes and replayed the scene at the liquor store. There was the store camera, aimed at the customers. It would not be able to get a good image of faces out on the street. Down the block was an autoteller, which the women could have passed by. Nothing on the street opposite the liquor store. No camera would have seen me walk up to them, or seen us walk back to the car.

"It's unlikely they will tie you to me from any video. If they thought I'd brought you here, we'd have gotten a call by now from the police. I think you're safe here."

"You don't get it, asshole. In three days, I'm going to need a party, and I'll be damned if it's going to be you. I can't stay here longer than that."

Cat looked pensive. "We have three days. Maybe four. Then we're out of here."

"Shit," said Becca. "This is just shit."

I decided not to mention that the housekeeper had seen them both here. If videos of the two were shown on the net, there was a chance she would see them. I went into the other room to send a few messages. There were some things I could do to limit the risks.

Dinner was in the media room, with an old movie playing. Becca sought out the chair furthest from me, but opposite, so she could watch my every move with a sullen glare. Cat had discovered the freezers, and was up and down during the whole movie, sampling fifty different ice cream flavors. She ended up asleep at Becca's feet before the movie ended, holding her overstuffed stomach.

After the movie, the room was quiet, and I rose from the couch silently to avoid waking her. Becca glared silently, and watched me leave the room. Upstairs in my bedroom, I considered closing the door. Not certain what I was expecting, I left it open.

§

Chapter Three

In the morning, I found Cat playing tennis on the autocourt. The machine was set to learning mode, gently returning each ball to where Cat could easily send it back over the net. I picked up a racquet and walked over to play doubles. The machine recognized me and hit a blistering return that I almost missed. The next one was lobbed easily to Cat. She hit it back ferociously, and the machine went into competition mode, no longer treating her like a beginner.

"So," she said, out of breath after twenty minutes of high energy play, "you didn't point out all the thousand reasons why Becca can't just walk out of here without any problem."

"She seemed to want a reason to stay," I admitted.

"She really does hate you, you know," she said, running a towel over her face.

"I'm not certain it's me she hates."

"Oh, be certain. Nothing you do or say will ever be right. She'll be waiting to pounce on anything you say. You're dirt, scum, something left on her shoe after walking through the dog park."

"And yet she's still here."

"Don't flatter yourself," she said, throwing the towel in the general direction of the towel rack.

I changed the subject. "I have an appointment in the city this morning. It'll take a few hours."

She brushed her hair back and turned towards me. "We don't need a babysitter or a playmate. You go do your thing. I haven't explored half this place yet."

Becca saw us in the hallway outside the media room. "Catrina! Look at all this shit the house let me buy with asshole's money!" Becca pointed at the screen. "What's your shoe size? They deliver all this stuff in one hour or your money back."

Cat looked over at me. "You go to your meeting. She'll be just fine until her guest budget runs out."

That could take some time, I thought.

§

Chapter Four

A man with money and no friends might be poorer than a man with friends and no money, but at least he can buy conversation. That's what psychiatrists are for. On this day I wasn't hurting for human contact, but this was a new shrink, my fourth, and cancelling the first appointment didn't seem wise. He might jump to some conclusion about my motives.

"I received all of your history from Dr. Maitland," he said, once I had settled into a comfortable chair. He sat in an identical chair, at an angle to mine, separated by a low table. "Of course, I'll never be able to view it all, but I had a rather long conversation with him."

"How's he doing these days," I said, conversationally.

"He says you have a habit of deliberately alienating people."

"He got a doctorate in psychiatry to figure that out?"

"You also have a doctorate in psychiatry, Jack," he said. "What have you figured out?"

"Mine doesn't count. I have eight doctorates. I get them out of Cracker Jack boxes. Just paper."

He thought for a while. "Do you feel you cheated in getting those diplomas? Because of your gifts?"

"You think what my father did to me was a gift?"

"Tell me about what your father did to you."

This part of the dialogue always bored me. But it was unavoidable. None of them wanted to just watch the videos of me telling the last guy. They thought the process was more important than the data.

My father developed SMTV, the technology that led to broad spectrum antivirals and ended almost all of the infectious diseases in the world, for those who could afford it. But the Somatic Mutation Transfer Virus could do much more than cure diseases. It allowed anyone to swap any gene in an organism for another gene, and ensure that only that gene was transferred, and that it was always in the right place and activated at the right time. He could cure genetic diseases by replacing the bad genes with good ones, either from a donor or from a synthetically produced strand of DNA.

It was after my brother was born that he got the idea to tinker with his children. There were laws against cloning humans, but no laws against modifying the genes in a zygote. My father collected gene sequences from tens of thousands of people. They came to the Xenocor clinics from all over the world to have little genetic defects fixed. He classified them by IQ, by athletic accomplishment, by beauty, by how well they accumulated worldly wealth. His computers selected gene sequences that correlated with success in every field. He studied the epigenetic information that up-regulated some genes and down-regulated others, and built a database of which genetic information led to success, and which led to failure. He had a large enough sample that environmental effects averaged out, leaving genetics as the sole discriminator of perfection.

It was too late for my brother. Good as the SMTV technology was, you could not replace every gene in every cell with a repaired one. There are trillions of them, and the error rates were never even close to that good. But you could do it for a fertilized egg. The egg that became me.

My father was very proud of himself. But he didn't stop there. I was sent to the best schools, had tutors and coaches, and everyone knew I was special, and could be pushed farther than other kids, that things came easy for me, and I had to have a highly enriched environment.

When I ran faster than all the other kids, it was expected, it was nothing special. When I got the best grades, I was given more work to do as a reward. When I could do everything much better than my older brother, I was told not to feel smug, because I had an advantage he didn't have. I never got the praise I saw him getting.

SMTV leaves markers. It's deliberate, so you can tell it worked right. You add some RNA keys and some green fluorescent protein and the cells light up where the genes have been replaced. They test for it in athletic competitions, like they do for performance enhancing drugs. I have a doctorate in genetics, of course, and I studied myself well. When I perform the test on my own cells, they light up like a Christmas tree. I can outrun any Olympic runner in any race, but I'll never win a medal. I can beat the best tennis player, but I'll never get the Wimbledon Cup.

But the worst part is the memory. I can't forget anything. All the little things that happen to a kid growing up, every hurtful word, every painful lesson about human relations, everything is there like it happened a moment ago. All the feelings, all the pain, all the frustration, all the times when I wanted to be proud of something I had done, but couldn't.

I notice things that other people don't. Somewhere in the back of my mind is a machine that records everything, and analyzes all the input, correlating and categorizing, sorting and filing. I know when people are bored with my conversation, or jealous, or intimidated, or hateful. I know when they are truthful, when they are hiding something. I know what they are going to say next half the time.

People irritate me.

So, who's alienating whom?

§

Chapter Five

The session ran later than I had expected. I got home well after noon. Cat and Becca were lying out in the sun by the side of the pool, in swimsuits they hadn't owned the day before. Cat sat up when I walked over.

"We had a nice long chat with your brother," she said. "Apparently the house won't let him in unless he uses his police override. You let perfect strangers have the run of the place, but your brother has to pull strings to get in the door?"

"You're claiming to be perfect? Or perfectly strange?"

"Don't you want to know what he said about you?" Cat said, ignoring my remark.

"I can imagine."

Becca seemed to want to have nothing to do with the conversation. She got up and dove into the pool, and began swimming laps.

Cat pointed to her. "She filled up three closets with crap she'll never wear. The house wouldn't tell us what the budget was. She kept trying to use it up. She's got a diamond ankle bracelet she won't take off."

"What did Sam say when he saw you two?"

"He thought there'd only be one of us. He also thought we'd have split by now. Said it broke your pattern."

I sat down. "What does he know about patterns?" I said, a little too loudly.

"He's smart. He has your dad's genes."

She was testing me. And at the same time making sure I knew what Sam had told them. I reclined in the lounge chair and considered how I felt about that. "He's smart. He's a damn good detective."

"He said he never had any trouble with kids in school, because his little brother would beat them up if they picked on him."

"He's my brother."

"How come you treat him like shit?"

"He's my brother."

Becca came out of the water and grabbed a towel. She worked at her hair quickly, then ran the towel down her body, but stopped at the ankle and gently patted the anklet there. She didn't notice I was watching.

"You're a little far from Maryland," I said, conversationally. Becca sneered at me. "We never said we were from Maryland."

"Your accents do. Not Baltimore though. Farther east."

Cat sat up. "Frederick," she affirmed.

"What brings you out here?"

"None of your business," Becca said, and turned to lie face down on the sun cot.

Cat looked over at her, then back to me. "Mom's out here somewhere."

"Your mother, or hers?"

"Both," she said, somewhat surprised.

I was surprised as well. "I would not have made you as sisters," I said.

"You wouldn't have made us, period, pervert," came a muffled reply from Becca, face down on the cot.

"Why not?" Cat asked.

I ticked off a list. "Facial bone structure, ratio of leg and arm bones to spine, adipose distribution, muscle striations indicating brown fat distribution differences, jaw line, tooth color," I said, "Those things generally go together in families, many from the maternal side. Cousins, maybe, but not the same mother."

"I remember when Becca was born. Visiting Mom in the hospital. You lose on this one, genius."

I let it go, and changed the subject slightly.

"You said 'out here somewhere'. I take it you haven't found her yet?"

Becca rolled over. "Let's talk about something else."

Cat and I were silent for a while. The Cat asked "So, how's your brother going to find out why the two guys were killed?"

I thought for a moment. "The nerve gas is the best lead. Not a lot of that around, or people who know how to make it, or people who know how to use it safely. Then there's always money — check the records of the liquor store, see if there was anything funny going on, see if the owner has income he can't explain. Check all the video cameras between the store and where they found the car. Canvas both areas, hoping to find a witness. I assume you were forthcoming when he questioned you?"

"He mostly wanted to ask about you. But we gave the description of what we saw, and what you told us you saw."

"He'll be checking out the car — where it came from, if it was stolen, if anyone saw it being stolen, when it was last charged."

"But none of that explains why he came here to see you," Cat said.

I looked at Cat. "He's just nosy."

"He cares about you."

I stood up. "I'll be in the gym. Missed my workout this morning."

§

Chapter Six

I had an unusually long workout. I had a lot of nervous energy to use up. By the time I came out of a long hot shower, the sun was going down. The house said Becca was in the media room watching a movie, and Cat was up in the observatory. I climbed the stairs.

The observatory is just a big glass room on the roof. The doors are always open during the day, so it doesn't act as a greenhouse, but at night it is a very pleasant place. Cat was on her stomach watching the sun set. The city lights were coming on, and the view was, as usual, spectacular. I knocked on the open door and waited to see if she was in the mood for company.

She rolled to her side and looked up at me. "So, the superman has a touchy spot."

"Apparently so does Becca," I countered. I sat down on the carpet next to her. She was quiet for a while.

"Mom left about a year after Bec was born. Becca was a surprise to Dad. Mom didn't tell him when she stopped using birth control. That wasn't why they broke up — they had been having a lot of problems and Mom thought a baby would fix things."

Cat paused for a moment. "I was born here in California, but Dad got a job in Maryland at one of the big biotech firms in Frederick. Becca was born there. After they split up, Mom couldn't handle living alone so far away from home. She came back here without us."

She looked over at me. "That's why Becca's messed up. She thinks Dad never wanted her, and Mom abandoned her. I've been protecting her all her life, and she hates that. Hates that I'm older and smarter and stronger and that dad loves me."

I digested that for a while. Cat stretched out and rolled onto her back. "So," she said, "That's why Becca doesn't like to talk about Mom."

"But you're out here to find her."

"We're out here to find out what she meant when she sent us a weird letter. And to get away from Dad. He's depressed when he's not on his meds, and really freaky when he is on them. Becca was a freshman in college when she got hooked on T. I dropped out a couple months before graduation so I could stay with her and keep her out of trouble. Dad was useless."

The sunset was fading, and the stars began to be visible through the transparent ceiling. I smelled cooking.

"Smells like Becca has decided to make dinner," I said.

"Oh shit!" Cat replied, and jumped up to rescue the kitchen.

§

Chapter Seven

The next morning, I overslept again. That usually happens when my subconscious is dealing with a lot of data, but nothing popped into my head upon waking, so maybe I was just tired. I could hear Cat and Becca's voices somewhere outside, but I could not make out any words.

No one bothered me during my workout, and the house was still empty when I went upstairs to work on a few ideas. For some of the inputs I would need to speak to my brother, but I could get a start on the search with what I had. Small amounts of very high value substances or objects that need to be kept cool or frozen, robberies committed with a shotgun under a long coat, shotgun murders in general, nerve agents, shipments of components of nerve agents, people with expertise in nerve agents, and counter measures and delivery systems for nerve agents. Specific details of which nerve agent was used would have to wait for Sammy's help.

I started another search. Catrina, Rebecca, biotech firms in and around Frederick Maryland, a date range, a divorce or separation, a move from the San Francisco Bay area to Frederick, incomplete college stay, durations one year, and three years, in the Frederick area. Inference searching takes much longer than keyword searching, and it can take days for the system to pull together little hints and associations into something concrete. But the name Jonathan Worthington came up right away. He had filed a missing persons report for his daughters Catrina and Rebecca in Frederick, Maryland. I let the search run, hoping to find something about his wife.

A polite tap on the door startled me, and I looked up to see Cat standing in the doorway. I waved her in.

"You might want to phone home, let your dad know you're all right," I said, pointing to the screen. She read the short news article, and then looked over at me.

"OK, so I'm not a natural blonde. But you knew that anyway."

"He's worried about you."

"That's nice. Finally. I have a friend in D.C. who has some postcards I left. She's going to start mailing them next week, so he thinks I'm still back on the east coast."

"What names did you give Sam when you talked to him? He'll have to report seeing you if the missing person report shows up in his witness file."

"We used Mom's maiden name. Jackson."

"That won't help a bit," I said. To demonstrate, I added "Catrina Jackson, Rebecca Jackson" to the search list, and the computer immediately did the association, and showed an article about Jonathan Worthington marrying Margaret Jackson. The separation papers followed.

"The police have access to much more information than my simple home computer. They won't need fancy correlation and inferencing software. I suspect your father has been notified that you were seen in the Bay Area. Sam would have left my address out of the report though."

I touched the exit mark on the screen, and it went dark.

From downstairs, Becca shouted up the stairwell. "Hey pervert, what are you hiding in the greenhouse?"

Cat looked up at me. "We've been exploring."

I walked to the door so I wouldn't have to shout, and looked down at Becca's face on the floor below. "It's hard to hide something in a glass building," I said, starting down the stairs. Cat followed.

"You said we could go anywhere we wanted. But the greenhouse is locked up. The house won't open the door." Becca gloated like she had found the dead bodies in a mystery game.

I smiled. "You'll like the greenhouse. My dad built it for his hobby. I loved it there when I was a kid."

"You grew up here?" Cat asked, puzzled.

"This is the house my parents built."

Becca looked over at Cat. "That explains why someone with no friends has a house with nine guest bedrooms."

We walked out of the house and across the wide lawn. The greenhouse was a set of connected buildings attached to a large glass-walled atrium. Condensation on the glass prevented a good view of the interior, but deep greens and occasional splashes of bright color hinted at flowering plants inside.

The big doors on the greenhouse are welded shut. The actual entrance is a normal sized door in the genetics lab. I led Cat and Becca around to it and it opened as we approached.

"You get in through the bathroom?" Becca asked.

"The greenhouse is a sterile workplace with negative air pressure contamination controls. Nothing gets in or out except people. The door will close behind us and the air will be filtered and sterilized while we shower in. When we're done showering, the far doors will open. There are coveralls in sterile wrap on the other side. I'm afraid they will be a little baggy on you two, but they have elastic on the hands and legs and waist so they should fit anyone. Scrub up well with the disinfectant. The doors won't open if the filters detect live bacteria or fungal spores."

There are four shower rooms, and I pointed to one of them while entering another. The women looked dubious, but stepped in. I closed my door, removed my clothes and stored them on the shelves of the changing room, and stepped into the shower. The glass door closed and the air filters pumped in a blast of ozone scented air and the ultraviolet lights came on. I started the shower, and lathered up with the disinfectant.

When the ultraviolet lights turned back off, the other door to the shower opened, and I stepped out into the air drier, which blasted me dry with warm air. I opened the plastic wrapping on a pair of coveralls and slipped in, pulling the booties around my feet and zipping up. I opened the final door into the genetic lab, and waited for Cat and Becca to come out of their door. I waited quite a while, but finally they entered, pulling on places on their coveralls where the elastic folds were uncomfortable.

The genetics lab is fairly austere. Built into the counter are small gene sequencers, expression analyzers, gene sequence assemblers, transcriptors, annotators, splicers and other common tools of the trade, along with sinks, a large refrigerator, an autoclave, and a case full of glassware, pipettes and whatnot.

The breathtaking part is the far wall, which is all glass, looking out into the greenhouse. Cat and Becca only glanced at the equipment, but could not take their eyes off the plants on the other side of the glass. I led them over to the sliding doors and into the greenhouse proper.

The greenhouse is humid, but cool, since none of the plants inside are tropical.

Becca was the first to speak. "This is totally cratered," she said, holding a large blossom gently in her hand. It was one of my father's striped tulips. A large yellow flower, it had stripes of blue spots spiraling around the outside of the petals.

"Dad was really proud of that one. Getting the spots to spiral that way across from one petal to the other and get smaller from base to tip was quite a challenge." Dad liked stripes a lot, and many of the plants had patterns of spots or lines on the leaves or petals. He had been studying how patterns are expressed in butterflies, tigers, tropical fish and the like, and had reproduced many of those patterns in his plants.

We walked through rows of green, splashed with wild colors, some flowers mottled in random splotches, others in precise patterns. Some were failures, yet too pretty not to keep. Others were less impressive to the eye, but proof of mastering subtle techniques of gene expression, such as the roses with the three-pointed thorns, or the vanilla scented pansies.

"Here's my first attempt," I said, pointing to a dome shaped mass of thick leaves. "I wanted to make a tree house. A house that grows like a tree. It's actually a bunch of vines that grow very thickly together, but only at the edges of an ethylene gradient provided by the little potted plant in the middle." I parted the thick leaves to show the perfect hollow dome of the inside, to show the little clay pot with a small succulent plant growing in it.

"I didn't think it was working at first. The air was never still enough to make a nice dome. But as the plants grew together and blocked the breeze, the parts that were too close died back and it ended up like this. It can be any size you want, but I've kept it this small out of nostalgia. I was eight years old when I created it, and that size still seems the right size to me."

"Which ones are yours and which are your father's?" Cat asked.

"He was into flowers," I said waving at the splashes of color. "I was into puns. The pea-shooter plant over there shoots its seeds about

20 feet. I could never get it to aim though. The leopard grass changes its spots from spring to winter. And the coco beans really do taste like coconut. Well, more of a macaroon, actually, too much vanilla."

"Why are they all locked up in here? Why don't you have them planted all around the house?" Becca asked.

"They can't survive outside. They need special nutrients, protection from ultraviolet, special hormones added to the water — there are 17 deliberate deficiencies bred into each one to make sure they can't propagate in the wild. Even so, we keep the air pressure low in the greenhouse so no pollens get outside. And the DNA is signed, so we can check for it in the wild, or tailor a virus to kill it if we have to."

Cat looked over at me. "How do you sign DNA?"

"It's just bits of information. You can encode anything you like in it. All these plants are signed by the creator, with the date, the lab notes, and a bunch of other information. It all shows up in the sequencer when you read the nucleotides."

"You use those machines in there to read that stuff?" Becca asked, looking back through the big window to the genetics lab.

"Yes. When I was a kid, I used to have fun putting bits of sandwich in the sequencer and looking at all the signatures. Most food is signed — the yeast and wheat in the bread, the lettuce, the tomato, peanut butter. You can read which companies developed that strain, when they did it, sometimes they even add company logos in machine readable file formats. If I wasn't careful about contamination, I'd get my own signature."

"Your DNA is signed?" Cat looked horrified.

"It's the law. Any changes made to an organism have to be signed and dated."

"That is just too raggin' weird," Becca declared.

"Half my DNA has SMTV tags, besides the signature. A few of the special genes are tagged by themselves, like the longevity genes from PureLife. Most of the really expensive genes are signed."

Cat held one of my long-haired grasses in her hand, stroking the soft fur. She looked up at me, then down at the plant, as if she was beginning to understand something. Then she brightened up and changed the subject.

"You're right, you know," she said cheerfully. "I do like the green-house."

We showered out of the genetics lab, dressed, and started back towards the house. Becca, as usual, kept as much distance from me as she could, running ahead, probably to hide in the media room again. I looked over at Cat.

"So," I said, "are you ready to talk about why you've chosen to hide away here for three days when you came out all this way to find your mother?"

"You mean like nobody kicked us out yet? We don't get to stay at many billionaire playgrounds where we live. The bathrooms here are as big as my house."

I waited for a better answer. Cat took her time, but the silence made her uncomfortable.

"Becca is afraid to meet Mom. She has this whole fantasy about what's going to happen, and she knows it isn't going to play out the ways she had it pictured. Mom is an alcoholic working at a liquor store, so it isn't going to be some fairy tale ending where everybody learns it was all some mistake and everybody loves everybody else again. It's going to really rag big time."

"Your mother works at a liquor store?"

"Yeah. We were scoping it out, late at night so she wouldn't be working, trying to get a feel for the whole thing, so we wouldn't have as many surprises. Plus, Becca was cribbing, and we couldn't meet Mom that way."

"Sam is going to shit when he finds out his witnesses are connected to the first homicide and didn't think to mention it," I predicted.

"So, we'll just make sure he doesn't find out," Cat said.

"This is Sammy, my brother. He's going to find out. I told you, he's a very good detective. One of us should give him a call before he does."

Cat looked down at the ground, and put one foot on the toe of the other. "I can do that," she said.

"First, though," I said, smiling, "you two get dressed up really nice. We're going out to dinner, after we make a few stops in town."

She looked down at her newly washed jeans. "This is all I have. Becca's the one buying all the fancy crap."

"OK then, we'll stop at Etienne's first, get you both something suitable. I don't think Becca's selections are exactly the impression we want to make tonight, but don't tell her I said so. We'll get expert help."

She hit me on the shoulder, hard. "No wonder you have no friends! You have the tact of a wart hog."

We took the limousine. I called Etienne's before we left, privately, ensuring they were apprised of our needs and would have people ready for us. When we arrived, an older woman introduced herself to the women as if she were an old friend of mine.

"Good afternoon, Jack. This must be Catrina and Rebecca, so good to meet you." She took each of the women by the hand. "My name is Grace. I understand you'll be needing some evening wear. Let me show you around. We have three collections today by three of my favorite designers, and we can have alterations done for you while you wait. And you know, it's the fashion to have your hair match the gown, not in color, of course, but in shape and cut, so I took the liberty of scheduling you both with Martina, she's my personal stylist, and does absolute wonders with hair." She reached to cup a handful of Becca's tresses, and said "She's going to just love your hair, dear, so many options."

Cat looked over at me, giving me a "what have you gotten me into" silent pantomime. I winked at her and said "You two will be a while. I'm going to duck out and run some errands for a bit. I'll be back in, oh, two, make that three hours." Grace was holding out three fingers behind her back where only I could see them.

I left the store, and walked out to the car.

My attorneys are used to dealing with me electronically for most things. We meet in private rarely, usually when the matter is a large financial transaction that would make it worth someone's while to bug my house or decrypt my communications. On such occasions, a walk in the park, or taking a small boat out on the lake passes a few billable hours in a pleasant way. This was the first time I had ever asked for a criminal lawyer to accompany us on such a walk, and Jacob had decided to bring some large men in suits to discreetly make sure we were not overheard.

They were waiting for the car when I arrived. The late afternoon sun was low over the small lake where a few sailboats and wind surfers made small wakes. We walked across the broad lawn towards the golf course, away from picnickers and the occasional skateboarder.

There was much to discuss, bringing Jacob, and the criminal lawyer he only referred to as Wilson, up to date on Cat and Becca, Jonathan Worthington, and Margaret Jackson, their connection to the murders, and my suspicions about motives and coincidences. Jacob had people who could make discreet inquiries, and keep an eye on individuals of interest, and we agreed on a course of action. Something was bothering me about Jonathan Worthington, and I needed more information, and I wanted to know if he stayed in Maryland or decided to come out west to find his daughters. Sam had surely notified him by now as to their whereabouts, although he probably didn't mention a specific address.

Eventually we ran out of things of interest to Wilson, and he departed to set things up. Jacob and I continued our walk. He asked how Sammy was doing, and whether Sam's wife would ever let me visit again after that affair with the dog and the drunk escort. I said it was unlikely, and probably just as well. First impressions are usually the most accurate.

We began walking back to the car, signaling that business was finished, and the suits closed ranks, one walking ahead of us, one well behind, and the rest just out of casual speaking range, but close enough to be there quickly if called. At the car, I thanked Jacob, nodded to the rest of the group, and got in. On the way back to Etienne's, I changed into my evening wear, somewhat awkwardly since it was impossible to stand up in the limousine.

At Etienne's, Grace met me at the door, ushered me inside, and straightened my bow-tie and smoothed wrinkles from my jacket, all in quick automatic gestures as we waited for Cat and Becca to come out front.

They came out together, Becca very self conscious in blue silk that flowed as she moved. Her hair swept across her brow and moved with the same liquid grace as the gown. She wore a diamond pendant on a thin platinum chain, and a matching bracelet. The other diamond was still on her ankle, setting off a pair of shoes the same color as the gown. Cat was dressed in red, left shoulder bare like a Greek archer. She had tiny ruby earrings, and shoes that made me think of Dorothy in Oz.

They were definitely ready to accompany James Bond to a casino on the Mediterranean.

Young men in suits rushed out to open the doors of the limousine, and we were on our way. Becca kept fingering the diamond on her neck. Cat pretended to be uncomfortable in the red dress, but was careful not to undo any of the special effects that had been done to her.

I own d'Artagnan's, and a table is always kept empty for me, although not always the same one. We entered by the ballroom, and the maître d'hôtel met us and escorted us past the small orchestra and the other guests to a small table next to some sound-deadening velvet drapery that kept conversations private and low volume. Heads turned to watch the women as they walked through the room, and Becca seemed to brighten with the attention. Cat was more interested in the room itself, with its high arched ceilings, chandeliers, and ice sculptures.

We went through the wine ritual, and then courses were brought one by one, often with a flourish, since I had encouraged the women to try some of the more flamboyant specialties, several of which involved flaming liqueurs and tableside final preparation.

"People are looking at me," Becca complained in a whisper.

"As well they should," I replied. "Grace would be insulted if they didn't."

"Check out these shoes," Cat said, holding a foot up gracefully. "They look like Cinderella, but I could run a marathon in them. They have arch support, cushioned soles, and they breathe like they aren't even there."

"You're registered at Etienne's under my account, in case you have other occasions you need to be prepared for. Feel free to take the car whenever you wish."

Becca looked at me suspiciously. "Why are you being so nice to us?"

I gave her a thoughtful look, glanced at Cat, and then back to Becca. "Perhaps I need the practice."

Cat looked at Becca. "Take advantage while it lasts. Tomorrow we can go get that yellow dress."

Becca brightened. She turned to me. "Grace wouldn't let me wear it tonight. She said it was for weddings and croquet parties. You wouldn't believe the feel of that fabric."

I smiled. "I have another meeting tomorrow morning," I said, pulling out my phone and tapping a quick note. "You can take the car over while I'm out. I'm making you an appointment. Shall I add 'yellow dress' to the note? I'm sure we can arrange a croquet party, if necessary."

Dessert menus arrived before either of them could answer. Becca declined, but Cat ordered the most decadent thing she could find, and asked for two forks. I declined as well, and Cat countered by ordering three forks. The sommelier arrived again, and we waved him away.

We watched dancers in the ballroom as we waited for dessert. "Downstairs the dancing is more contemporary," I said. "In case you're bored some evening."

Cat looked over at me. "How long are you planning on entertaining us at Jack's Castle? We could never get in a place like this without you there."

"I wouldn't worry," I said. "I know the owner, I'm sure he'd be happy to add you to the A list. And downstairs they allow jeans and yellow dresses."

We finished dessert, much contented, and got up to leave.

In the car on the way home, Cat asked "So tell me something. Why does your brother work at the police station? Did he get stiffed out of the will or something?"

"No, he owns most of Xenocor. He just hates the business. He got into police work after Dad was shot."

Becca came out of her pensive reverie. "Someone shot your father?"

"You can read all about it on the net. Dad died the next morning. A professional hit. They never found the guy."

"Why did they shoot him?" Becca seemed upset.

"A lot of companies used to make a lot of money treating diseases instead of curing them. If you have an incurable disease that can be kept at bay by taking a daily pill, you'll pay a lot for that pill. A broad-spectrum universal antiviral makes all that money go away. But there were a lot of other people upset. Religious nuts who saw what would happen when all sexually transmitted diseases had cures. People worried about overpopulation, people against genetic engineering. There was a long list of people who had reasons for wanting Dad dead. In the end, it was too late. The genie was out of the bottle, and Xenocor was the cork, flying higher and higher. And Sammy could afford anything he wanted, and he wanted to be a detective."

I was tired when we arrived home. Becca and Cat were still excited from their evening out. As I started up the stairs, I reminded Cat: "Call Sam. Tonight." She sobered quickly, and nodded assent.

The next morning, I was almost late for my shrink appointment. I should not have scheduled them so close together, but it seemed like a good idea at the time. Break the new guy in, get him up to speed, see if he still wants the job after a few meetings with yours truly. Some don't, and why waste time?

But now that I didn't need someone else to talk to, I was stuck with the schedule. I could cancel, but that wouldn't be me. Easy enough to just do what I had committed to do. Or maybe I was just used to following through.

There was still no flash of insight when I awoke. My subconscious pattern recognizer was working overtime, and still had come up with nothing. But apparently there was something important to work out, and it insisted on the extra sleep. I figured it was something to do with the women, but it could also be something to do with the murders. Something wasn't right, and my brain was going to work on it until it either solved it by brute force, or got enough new information to work it out.

In the meantime, I was skipping breakfast and rushing out to go talk to someone I didn't want to talk to instead of staying at home talking with someone I really wanted to talk to some more. But hey, even I can't feel sorry for me. Spoiled rich kid with the best genes money can buy. Richard Corey was an idiot.

As it was, I arrived a few minutes early. Doctor Hoffman's receptionist smiled at me and pushed a button when I came in. I assumed this lit up something on the doctor's monitor in the other room. She looked like she would have spoken to me, but someone had warned her against it. She found something important to do in the file drawer while I waited.

The door to the doctor's office opened, and he beckoned me in. I said "Oh, no, not the comfy chair!" but he did not seem to understand the reference. I get that a lot. You can never tell what people have seen, what they notice, what they remember, what they forget. Unless it's me, then you know it's everything, everything, everything, and nothing.

"Do you have a problem with comfortable chairs?" he asked.

"Just a bad joke, a hundred and seventeen years too late," I said.

He seemed interested at that, and touched a pad on his desk. Making a note of something interesting in the recording.

"What would you like to talk about?" I asked, before he could. People love to talk about themselves. They are taught to rein that in, to listen to others talk about themselves. One reason psychiatry pays as well as it does is that psychiatrists insist that you talk about yourself. That's why you pay them. Everybody wins.

Hoffman apparently had a list of questions he wanted to ask, and was having trouble deciding which to go with first. So, he struck to the cliché.

"How old were you when your mother died?" he asked.

"Two years, seven months, five days, nine hours. The minutes are a little unclear — no one knows exactly when her heart stopped."

"You seem a little cavalier about the subject," he said. I could read the movement of his eyebrow in two different ways. I chose challenging.

"I remember every detail of every day of my life. Some days I'd like to forget. But I'm stuck with them. But after living them over again a few thousand times, you learn to cope. I'm coping. You ask a question designed to bring that memory to the forefront, and I find a way to answer it with unemotional data. I've already cried those tears."

And I would again. Just not today.

"It was a car accident, wasn't it? Is that when your face was damaged?"

Someone had told him not to pull any punches. I must have really pissed off Doctor Maitland.

"It was a car accident. I was at home. The face happened later."

"Perhaps you'd like to tell me about that, then," he said, doing the eyebrow thing again.

I paused. I can read off from memory exactly the words I used when explaining this before, to other people, or other shrinks. But when I do that, it's boring. Boring to me, and that shows in my voice. Besides, if he wanted that, he'd have viewed the recordings from Maitland. Maybe he had. I'd be able to tell from his face when I started talking. I approached the subject from a direction I had never used before.

"I got in my first fight when I was a little over five years old. Broke an eight-year-old's jaw. I got into a whole lot of trouble. I was much stronger than he was, and I was smart enough to know better than to break his jaw. At least that's what Dad said. I knew exactly what I was doing, and why, I just had not yet had enough experience to foresee the consequences."

Hoffman waited for me to finish.

"The next time I got into a fight, I went for maximum pain without leaving any marks. But first I had to make sure that the other guy got in some good punches, black eye, bloody nose, cuts on the face. That worked out much better. The other guy got in trouble. And he never wanted to get in a fight again. And he never bothered Sammy again. I got in a lot of fights in school. Never the same guy twice."

"But you never got reconstructive surgery. The broken nose, the scars, the broken cheekbone, all of that is fairly easily repaired by a skilled surgeon," he explained, as if I needed to be told.

I looked at him and copied his eyebrow affectation. "Do you think I have a self esteem problem? Something that would go away if I made myself pretty again? I am probably the richest, strongest, smartest man you're ever likely to meet. What do I need with one more advantage over the rest of you?"

He pressed something on his desk again. And he had seen Maitland's videos. Probably spent the last two days with them. He leaned forward.

"So, the face, the hostility, these are your way of handicapping yourself, to better fit in with the rest of us mere mortals?"

"Touché. But we both know I think it would take a lot more than that. I think even you think that. But I would, wouldn't I?"

Hoffman studied me quietly for a moment.

"There are two psychiatrists in the room. One is smarter than the other, and got perfect grades, and wrote seventeen groundbreaking papers, some of which are used to this day to teach new psychiatrists. But that one is in the comfy chair asking me for my help. What can I do for you, Doctor Wright?"

I opened my mouth to answer, then shut it. Why was I about to tell the fourth best shrink on the west coast what I had never told the best three? Had something changed in me? Had he figured something out that they had missed? It was simpler than that. They had never asked.

I looked over at Doctor Hoffman. "I want you to make it stop hurting."

§

Chapter Eight

Sam arrived at the house shortly after I returned. Cat's idea of cooking was ordering a pizza. We were finishing lunch when the house announced his approach. Cat looked over at me as if ready to duck. "I guess he got my message."

I opened the door personally. Sam has his official business face on, but gave up on it as soon as he crossed the threshold. "Hi J.T.", he said, looking past me at the two faces hanging back in the hallway. Sam never used the front entrance either.

I think we had all been expecting the volcanic tempered foul-mouthed Sam, but he was a subdued, concerned Sam this afternoon, and none of us knew what to do with that Sam.

"We've been looking for Margaret Jackson all morning," he said quietly, looking from Cat to Becca and back. "She was last seen the morning after the shooting. She had come in to work, saw the police tape and squad cars, and went in through the manager's entrance in the back, using her access card. An officer had to stop her from crossing the tape line to get something from a freezer. The officer told her to stay put and wait for a detective, but apparently, she disappeared after he finished dealing with some gawkers in the front. No one has seen her enter her apartment, and her car was left in the store parking lot."

Cat studied his face. "Where does she live? We only have her work address."

"South City, a block of apartments on Industrial. Subsidized housing, not one of the better parts of town. I'd recommend against any ideas you have of paying a visit there. We have the place on video 24/7, so we'll know if she shows up."

Becca was concerned. "Do you think she's OK?"

"We're looking for her as a possible material witness, but it's beginning to look like she's involved in some way," Sam said quietly.

"Involved how?" Cat asked.

"That freezer was the one Roland Drake broke into after shooting the night clerk. The only thing he took from the store was something from that freezer in a small brown paper bag. Margaret Jackson may be the only person alive who knows what was in that bag, apart from the people who killed Roland Drake with AC 13 binary nerve agent."

Sam had been looking directly at me when he mentioned the name of the toxin. He knew what I could do with that information that the systems at the police station could not.

He looked back to Cat. "This brings us to the rather serious matter of some information that was withheld until I received a rather terse message from you last night. You need to tell me everything about your recent communications with Margaret Jackson, and any involvements with her or her associates prior to the night of the shooting."

He was all official business Sam again, never referring to the woman as Cat and Becca's mother, and letting it be clear that serious consequences would arise if any more surprises showed up after he left.

Becca started first. "We didn't believe her. She's always doing flakey shit, messing with Dad's head, calling in the middle of the night and hanging up, all kinds of shit. We thought this was one more time."

Cat interrupted. "But Dad was messed up and being a total rag, he'd fucked up his meds again and was scaring Becca, so we flagged out. Paid this trucker chick for a ride all the way to Barstow, and then shared driving with these two guys going back to Berkeley."

Sam broke in. "What was it you didn't believe?"

"It was a video she left on the phone, for me," Becca said. "It was some weird shit, like 'I have proof of what Jon did to Catrina.'"

"She said it was too dangerous to move it right then," Cat took up. "She said something like 'a lot of powerful people want it kept quiet.' All that melodramatic cops and spies shit. She was drunk, she could barely find the send button."

"We spent the night on the roof of the supermarket. So that we wouldn't get hassled," Becca chimed in, picking up the earlier time-line.

"She sent the vid from the store, so we had the address," Cat explained. "We waited until late because we figured they wouldn't have an old lady working nights in a place like that. But Becca was feeling really bad," she looked up at me quickly, "and then Jack came along and the guy shot the other guy and we all flagged out of there in Jack's car."

Sam was recording all of this. "What was it that Jonathan Worthington did to Catrina?"

"Nothing!" said Cat. "That's why we knew it was goat. Dad never, ever, laid a hand on me in his life, never got weird, never did anything like that. He had his problems, but they were all about him, he never hurt anyone."

Sam looked at Becca for confirmation. "Dad always loved Cat," she said. "I mean as a daughter. He'd never hurt her, or do anything nasty. Mom was just milking goat."

Sam looked at his phone. "For the record, and since I am not familiar with the phrase, could you explain that last part?"

Cat explained. "Milking goat. What Becca does to Jack. What Jack does to you. Says shit to make you mad. Push your buttons."

Sam pursued that. "Was child abuse one of Jonathan Worthington's buttons?"

Becca looked puzzled. "No. If she wanted him torqued, she would usually mention his problem. He deals with it the best he can, but they don't have good meds for that yet."

"What problem is that?" Sam asked.

"Hinshaw Barnes," Cat said. "His mom and his dad were both carriers, so he has it full blown. That's why he was so ragged at Mom when Becca was born natural. Without in-vitro selection, she'd have a fifty percent chance of being a carrier. Carriers can have problems too, once they're old enough."

"Cat's clean," Becca said. "She was selected."

"Becca doesn't want to know. What's the point of testing if you can't do anything about it?"

Sam looked puzzled. "If it's genetic, why not just fix it?"

Time for me to speak up. "Hinshaw Barnes is a brain disorder that forms in-utero. After the fourth week, intervention has no effect."

No one said anything for a while. Sam's phone kept recording. He seemed to be cataloguing all the bits of information he'd just heard.

"So, Margaret Jackson had something she thought was proof of something Jonathan Worthington had done to Catrina Worthington. She kept it in a small paper bag in a freezer at her place of employment. A freezer that was in the back and normally locked and unavailable to customers. Roland Drake knew where to look, or the clerk told him where to look at gunpoint. Drake felt it necessary to kill the clerk after he had secured the bag, or after he had the location of the bag. Margaret Jackson is missing, either voluntarily to avoid arrest or to avoid Drake, or she has met with Drake's accomplices." Sam looked at Becca as he said this last part. She understood the low chances of surviving such a meeting.

Sam continued. "The question is, what is small enough to fit in a paper bag, requires refrigeration, and is worth the lives of two or more people?"

I caught Sam's eye. "Evidence," I said.

"Of something Jonathan Worthington did to Catrina Worthington." Sam said.

"Of something illegal, related to something Margaret Jackson thought her husband had done to Cat," I corrected. "Biological evidence, most likely."

"Evidence which is most likely destroyed at the moment, by someone with access to military nerve agents." Sam looked over at Cat. "Do you have any idea where your mother may have gone to hide? We've had no luck at shelters, transportation, cash dispenser video, net access or phone calls. Where would she go if she was in trouble?"

"She could go to Dad," Becca suggested.

"She must have friends here," Cat said.

"We have people canvassing her phone contacts and net records. If she's with someone local she has electronic correspondence with, we'll find her. But if she's evading arrest, she will know not to go there."

Sam closed the phone and stood up, stretching his legs. "That's all for the official record. If it's all right with you ladies, I'd like to have a private discussion with Jack."

No one answered, and Sam nodded his head to the back door, and we walked out onto the wide lawn.

"They don't seem to have seen the side of you we've all grown to love," Sam said, when we were clearly out of earshot of the house. "Five days. Is that a record? All this other shit, I could handle that and toss it off as coincidence. But there's something else going on you're not telling me. I can't have you stonewalling a double homicide investigation."

I had been expecting this. I had actually thought about it, thought about bringing it up with Hoffman. I was always open with my brother. That's the cause of most of our troubles.

"Becca's like any of the rest of you controls," I said, using the term I knew would 'milk his goat'. "If she wasn't trying so hard to annoy me all the time, she might actually piss me off like the rest of you do. But Cat rings alarm bells somewhere deep. There's something really out of place, and my hind brain thinks it's really important, but can't resolve it yet. It's a feeling like I'm sailing off the end of the world and the rigging is too tangled to steer away. I have to unravel the knot. But there's also the fact that she doesn't have all the little affectations you all have that drive me nuts. She never repeats anything. It's like she knows what it's like to be me. And that scares the shit out of me."

"You like her." It was a statement.

"Is that what it's like?" I asked.

"Probably not for us controls," he said. "But I like a lot of people, it's not a scary new experience."

We reached where he'd parked his car. He turned to me and smiled as he opened the door. "Take care of yourself."

"You too, Sammy. Tell the dog I'm sorry."

"Fuck the dog, asshole. Tell Catherine you're sorry." He slammed the door and drove away.

§

Chapter Nine

Back in the house, I went upstairs to set up some searches. AC 13 was a binary nerve agent I had never heard of before. There was a lot to read, and I was not a chemist, so there was a lot to learn before I could make sense of what I was reading. It was an hour and a half before I could put together the right pieces for the query.

Binary nerve agents are designed to be easy to handle safely. You need two parts to be dangerous. In the case of AC 13, the catalyst is a small molecule with a residence half life of a few days in the bloodstream. A milligram would be flushed out to ineffective levels in about three weeks. It was tasteless, and absorbed by membranes in the nose and throat. It could be added to food or drink, or sprayed on like a perfume, or used as an aerosol over large populations.

The second part is harmless without the catalyst. Contact with body parts containing the catalyst leads to a fast reaction that creates a highly toxic molecule that shuts down nerves in the heart, lungs, and the brain if it is inhaled. Skin contact with the product molecule causes convulsions and coma, leading to death if not treated within a couple hours. But in the person actually carrying the catalyst, death happens in seconds, often in the same breath.

By examining the body, the police lab could determine both when the death occurred, and when the catalyst had been administered. That would establish a window of time that might be useful to an inference engine like mine, or the one Sam used in his work.

It is unlikely that the second assailant went out and bought some ready-made AC 13, or stole some from some military munitions factory. It is proscribed by chemical weapons treaties, and none is supposed to be made or stockpiled anywhere. It is more likely that someone made it, and probably locally. A search for chemical weapons specialists on the west coast was pending, but it would probably never bear fruit. That is not often listed on job resumes.

The precursor chemicals include several that are used in insecticide manufacture. This was more likely to yield something useful. There are four different ways to get to the final product, each with different starting materials and procedures. I started a search for any discussions of those ingredients and the more common reagents used in the process. This would take a while, because I could not use any public indexes or my searches themselves could be searched. But I had a few petabytes of the most trafficked net data in the cache here at home, and that would give the inference engine enough of a lead to go spidering out the data not yet cached.

Next was the equipment needed for manufacturing the two parts of the binary toxin. A reasonable person would manufacture each part in separate buildings. I added these items to the search model. If I were manufacturing this stuff, I would want to know if I had accidentally ingested or inhaled one of the components, so I could make sure I did not subsequently come in contact with the other. One way to do this was to become allergic to both compounds. This I knew how to do. Would the chemist also know how to manipulate the immune system with custom proteins? It seemed like a long shot, but I decided to visit the greenhouse in the morning and work out the sequences needed, and then add them to the watch list. If someone ordered up that custom protein from Xenocor, we'd have them. Unfortunately, there are dozens of other companies that did that kind of work. If the chemist was on a budget, he might be asking for competitive bids, though, and we might get lucky.

An olfactory response might be more comfortable than a rash. If I trained my nose to respond to the chemical by simultaneously smelling two odors not likely to be associated with one another, say almond oil and a gas leak, then I would know to stay away from the other chemical. Such olfactory training is common in many industries, and while expensive, a simple nasal spray can allow a baker to know when the perfect sourdough starter had ripened. I brought up a list of companies that provide that service. A discreet inquiry to the sales office, with enough incentive, and I might find out if any such sprays had been made for those two targets. In the meantime, I could create my own the slow way, by modifying the genes in some yeast. It would take a day or two to get ready.

I turned my attention to financial matters for another hour and a half, and then went downstairs to teach Cat how to make Chicken Marsala for dinner. Something in me had decided that her education had to expand beyond microwave ovens and pizza delivery.

§

Chapter Ten

The next morning, I was in the gym, bench pressing, when Cat knocked gently at the open door. Surprisingly, Becca was behind her, avoiding my eye. Cat was dressed for a workout. Becca, on the other hand, was ready for Cinderella's ball. She'd been experimenting with her hair, and had come up with something surprisingly subtle and effective. Cat came into the gym as I continued exercising.

"I have a question," Cat said. I continued pushing the weights up and down slowly, not answering the statement, but waiting for the actual question. She continued.

"All that equipment in the greenhouse, all that gene stuff. Does it work on people?"

"You want to have polka dot striped skin?" I asked.

Becca snorted, and Cat giggled. "Can you read our genes?"

"The sequencer can," I said, lifting the weights up. "That takes a while. But the mapper can show you if you have any of the major known genetic disorders. That takes about ten minutes." I let the weights down again.

"Can it tell if Becca has the same mother as me?"

I had the weights up about halfway. I put them back down, and sat up.

"You don't. I already told you that."

"We don't believe you," Becca said.

I stood up and wiped sweat off my face with a towel.

"We can sequence you both, and compare the results. Or we can just sequence the 37 genes in your mitochondria, since those are inherited from the mother only. That would tell us if you both came from the same egg donor. That's a lot faster. Faster still is to use the mapper to see which genetic flaws you both share. All of the mitochondrial ones should be the same, and there should be little difference in the others, if you share the same parents."

"Are needles involved?" Becca asked.

"No needles. A cotton swab in the mouth, and then you wait. It'll take longer to shower in than to get the mapper results."

"Let's go, " said Becca. "You need the shower anyway."

Foregoing the rest of my workout, I followed Becca to the door to the pool, then out across the grass to the greenhouse. Cat kept by my side, a little close. I could tell that this was primarily Becca's idea, and that Cat was a little uncertain.

At the greenhouse, Becca had already closed the shower door behind her. I opened another shower door, and stepped in. I was about to close it when Cat slipped in with me, and closed it after her. I said nothing, and started removing my clothes. We shared the showerhead, alternating between soaping and rinsing. I admired her athletic body quietly, and wondered if the two had conspired on this part of the experiment. As I worked shampoo into my hair with my eyes closed, Cat began scrubbing my back. After I had rinsed, I did the same for her.

We unwrapped the coveralls and put them on, and then stepped through into the genetics lab. Becca was facing away from the door as we entered, looking out into the greenhouse, and did not turn around until we moved over to the sink. I took that as confirmation of a conspiracy, and smiled.

I opened the case above the sink and removed a pack of cotton swabs, handing them each one. I took one myself, and demonstrated the technique, rubbing the swab against the inside of my cheek, then pulling the swab down into its plastic sleeve, and flipping on the cap. The women did the same, and I marked mine with my name and handed Becca the pen. She signed hers, and handed the pen to Cat.

"It doesn't really matter," I said, "We can easily tell where each sample came from, but this is the normal protocol." Cat signed hers.

I pressed the button on the sequencer to open the tray, and we each put our samples inside. Pushing the button again, the tray slid back into the machine, and locked, and the display lit up.

"That will take a while," I said. "The mapper is even easier." I went over to the mapper and opened the case above it. I pulled out three small vials. I held one up to my mouth and filled it with saliva, then flipped its plastic cap closed.

"Just spit and close it up," I said, handing one to each of them. I placed mine in the slot in the mapper, and collected the others. I put a fresh mapping gel in the cartridge, and started the machine.

"This is going to tell us what genetic defects you have?" Becca asked with a smirk.

"And it will find some," I said. "There are a few dozen that weren't known at the time of my conception." The machine ejected the sample into the autoclave, and opened up for the next one. I loaded Becca's into the machine, put in another gel, and started it up again. As it was working, I brought up the results of my sample.

"Here we go, " I said, pointing to the display. "This one is associated with dry skin. This one here means that my fingernails grow just a little bit slower than most people." There were several more, but with symptoms much harder to explain.

"Where's the arrogance gene?" Becca asked sarcastically.

"That one is not considered a defect," I deadpanned. The machine ejected Becca's sample, and opened for Cat's. I placed it in, and put in the third gel. As it worked, I brought up Becca's results.

"Rag out!" Becca said in dismay. Page after page of results filled the display.

I looked at the display. "That's about what I'd expect from a normal control. There are 1,048,576 loci detected by each gel. There's an error rate of about point zero two percent, which we'll correct for when we have the sequence data. That alone counts for a little over two hundred of these. We could eliminate them by running the test a few more times, and only including the ones that match in four out of five runs. That would leave a bit over seven hundred good hits. Most controls will run between six hundred and four-teen hundred hits, so you're on the low side, actually."

Cat looked over at me. "How come yours didn't show two hundred errors?"

"I always use myself as a control, because I have mine in memory. Both in my head and in the machine. The machine is looking at several hundred runs for my samples, and the error rate goes way down."

The machine ejected Cat's sample, but I kept Becca's up on the dis-play. "Do you want me to interpret some of this for you?" I asked Becca. She looked up at me, meeting my eyes for the first time to-day.

"Sure. Tell me all about what's wrong with me," she said, dejected.

I stepped over to the display. "Let's go the other direction," I said, touching the display. It blanked, showing a single line that said "0 entries".

"Of all the known genetic causes of reduced mental capacity, you have none," I said. I touched the screen again. It showed seven lines. "These are the ones that might result in a shorter life expectancy. This one says you should start taking a cholesterol control sequence about the time you reach menopause to prevent it from shortening your lifespan. This one says to avoid inhaling fumes from a certain industrial solvent. But that one's been outlawed. There's a simple way of eliminating all of these either through diet or an intervention, and I'm sure all of these are in your medical records already, and you've probably been made aware of them at some time."

I touched the screen again, and the full list came back up. Selecting one at random, I touched it. The screen filled with a description of the trait, its frequency in the population, and other information. "This one is all about a sensitivity to paraaminobenzoic acid. So don't use it as a sunscreen. Half the people in the world have this trait, mostly anyone with European descent."

I went back to the full list, and picked another one at random, expanding it. "This one says you have fewer bitter taste buds than average. So certain foods taste better to you than to most people. Broccoli perhaps. About forty percent of the population has this trait."

"Where's the gene for being bad at math?" she asked.

"You don't have any of them. You can't blame your genes. If you work at it as hard as most people, you'll do as well as they do. Work harder, you'll do better."

She hesitated. Then asked "How about for alcoholism and depression?"

I touched the screen a few more times. The list was a couple pages long. I touched the first one. "The highest priority is this one." I read silently at the expanded view. "It's treatable. Associated with exposure to light at the right time of day, treatable with several inexpensive pharmaceuticals. But wear blue blocking sun glasses when you are in artificial light after dark, and it will never be a problem."

I expanded the second one on the list. "Here's one associated with risk taking. Personally, I'd keep that one. It's generally associated with success in a number of areas, from starting a business to selecting a mate. Helps you recognize opportunities instead of fearing them."

I selected the third one on the list. "Here is why that one showed up as a problem. This is a dopamine shift antagonist. That means drugs that stimulate pleasure centers work better in you than in most people. It's generally associated with addictive behavior."

"We knew that already," Becca said.

"Actually," I said, "you're missing most of the worst ones in that regard. The combination of these two is still rated low in likelihood of causing problems. You may not have your genes to blame for your drug habit."

"How about all my other problems? How come I'm not pretty, or tall, or smart, or popular? How come I had braces and Cat never did? How come?" She had a quaver in her voice, but she was not giving in to tears.

"You're not pretty because you don't smile enough," I said. "The bone structure is excellent, the skin tone, the symmetry, the color. The problem is behavioral. I don't have a feel for popularity, I haven't seen you in enough social situations, but I suspect the same is true there. Decide to like people, and they'll like you back. The height is genetic." I touched the screen. "Here are seven markers for height, and you have none of the ones for dangerously fast growth. These seven are associated with below average height, but there are hundreds of height traits, and seven low ones means you are about average height. And you are. This mapper is for genes that cause problems, so it won't show most of the good genes for height, which you probably have. We'll wait for the sequence data to confirm that."

I went back to the main list, and set up another filter. Five lines showed up. "These are the genes associated with problems in tooth growth or location. You can blame the braces on your genes. You'll probably pass those on to your kids, and they will have braces too. Smile for me," I said, looking at her mouth. She grimaced mockingly. I looked at her teeth. "Problem solved," I said.

She looked at me, defiant. "So why can't I be happy?" she challenged.

I looked down at her, then over to the computer screen, then back to her.

"Becca," I said softly, "DNA is not destiny. There's nothing here that indicates a genetic problem. What is here is all either treatable or trivial. You're normal. Life has thrown you some curves, and may have caused you to doubt yourself, but that can be handled as well. I know someone who is famous for helping people that way. I'm sure he'd love to have a chat with you, help you sort things out. He can also help you through the addiction if you like. He's the best on the west coast, and I think he'd like you."

"This friend of yours, is he a shrink?" Becca sneered.

"He's no friend. He hates my guts. But he loves my money. I worked with him for a couple years. Yes, he's a psychiatrist. I learned a lot as a patient of his."

"What did he cure *you* of?" she asked.

"Nothing," I said. "He thought my problem was psychological, but in my case it's genetic. In my case, everything's genetic."

Cat spoke up. "Is mine ready?"

I turned to the screen, and pulled up her results. A list of a little over 300 lines showed on the screen.

"This is wrong," I said, looking at the data. "Something screwed up, we'll have to do this one again."

I got down another couple of sample containers, and handed one to Cat. I filled mine and placed it in the machine. When the sample was ejected, I pulled up my results and started her sample processing. My results showed the same data as before. No problem with the machine.

Cat's second sample was ejected, and I pulled up the data from the two tests. The list was even shorter than before.

"The two runs are both screwy," I said. I selected a filter for mitochondrial DNA, and compared Becca's data to Cat's. "If we could trust Cat's run, which we can't, then this would be the answer you came here for. Becca has two minor mitochondrial hits, affecting metabolism and endurance, but only slightly. Cat has neither. The mitochondrial match should have been complete, if you have the same mother."

"But you can't trust mine?" Cat asked.

"No. Look at Becca's mitochondrial results," I said, pulling up the filtered results. There were two pages of hits. "This is what we would expect. This is normal. Now look at Cat's results." I filtered Cat's data, and the "0 entries" result showed up.

"For some reason, the machine is missing most of Cat's variability. It must be some software glitch. Something data dependent, since my results and Becca's are what we would expect."

I pulled up the full results from Cat again. I didn't need to look a second time, my memory had it recorded already. But something in the back of my mind was raising red flags, and wanted me to focus on this data. There was something here I needed to notice. I wasn't seeing it.

I expanded the first entry. "This is a subtle one," I said to Cat. "I remember reading about this one when it was found, just a couple years ago. Most of the genes on the gel were discovered before I was born. This one is associated with long term studies in mice, over generations. A tendency for the chromosome to break at this spot a little more often than normal. Not a big deal, just a slightly higher chance of a crossover event that might put two genes together where one won't get methylated properly. I have this same trait in me." I pulled up my results and pointed to the same line.

Cat and I shared four traits. Normally, this would not be a big deal. But I had less than thirty, instead of several hundred. This was pushing coincidence into a place it never goes.

"I think I see the problem," I said. "The machine is only showing results for traits found after a certain time. Clearly a software problem." I sorted Cat's results by date of discovery, and pointed to the oldest one.

"I was barely a year old," Cat said. My face felt warm, and I could feel my heart beating faster than normal. My subconscious was beating at my door. This was it. I looked over at Cat.

"There's a test I'd like to run," I said. "Can I get another cheek swab from you?" I walked back to the cabinet and took down two swabs. I swabbed my mouth, and Cat swabbed hers. I put mine into the trace reader, and its display quickly came up with hundreds of pages of data. I put Cat's swab into the machine, and held my breath.

The display simply said "No signatures found." I touched the screen. The display changed to "No markers found." I let out my breath, feeling foolish.

"Well, that rules out the weirdest possibility," I said. "No one has been tinkering with your DNA. It looks like I'll have to have the machine checked out."

"What was all of that stuff on the first set?" Cat asked.

"That was my sample. Those were all the signatures of the changes made to my genes, and all the markers for SMTV, one for each modification. You don't have any signatures, and you don't have any SMTV markers. You're a clean control. So, we wait for tomorrow and read the sequence data, to find out what the mapper missed."

"But we still don't know if Cat and I have the same mother," Becca said.

I thought for a bit. "We still have my father's old sequencer. It's a lot slower, but we can just have it scan the mitochondrial DNA, and then compare that way. We'll have the results sometime after lunch."

It took a while to prepare the samples for the older sequencer. Not only was it an ancient machine, but we had to select for plasmid loops, so that only the mitochondrial DNA would be sequenced. It was half an hour later when I was ready to start the run. I set the machine to run both samples sequentially, and considered just waiting there in the lab for it to complete, but I was getting hungry, and I figured the two women were as well. And since we hadn't opened the door to the greenhouse proper, we would not have to shower out. Before leaving the lab, I filled the yeast brewer with nutrients, and ran the program I had set up earlier to make the olfactory sensor.

I didn't bother to change out of the paper coverall. I collected my sterilized gym clothes, and walked out into the sunshine. Cat came out a few minutes later, dressed in her workout clothes. Becca took a lot longer. She came out with her hair pulled back and her party dress on, and caught my glance. She curtsied, and flashed a big fake grimace of a smile at me that disappeared as quickly as it came. She avoided my eyes after that, and walked quickly back to the house. Cat and I walked more slowly.

"You were pretty blunt back there," Cat said.

"That's my nature."

"I think it worked. Having her face slapped with it, I mean. I saw her face. She was listening. She never listens to me."

"Why be subtle?" I asked. "According to you, she already hates me."

"That part about the help with the addiction. Can someone really help her? She's starting to crib already. Another day or two, and she'll be full blown."

"He can help with the withdrawal. The physical part anyway. The dopamine system is pretty well mapped out, and the treatments work. But it will be up to her. We can't make her do it."

"I'll talk to her. She really doesn't want to go out there and hook up again." Cat stopped and reached for my arm. I turned to face her. "Thanks," she said, her eyes locked on mine. She kissed me on the shoulder, and hurried ahead of me into the house.

I watched her run, taking my time and walking slowly on the thick grass.

I went upstairs to change. When I came down, Cat and Becca were making sandwiches. The kitchen counter was covered with sliced meats, cheese, lettuce, tomatoes, sliced pickles in several varieties, four different kinds of bread, and all the condiments they could find from the refrigerator and the pantry. Cat was slicing tomatoes. Becca was shredding lettuce into fine threads.

"Whadayalike big boy," Cat called as I entered the room. "I was the fastest assembler at Crestmont Super Subs, and I can make any meal on the menu in 3 minutes flat or your money back. Double that if you want it toasted, though, this toaster is slow as whaleshit drifting to the bottom of the ocean."

"Surprise me," I said. "Whatever your favorite is."

Becca giggled. "That'll surprise him, all right."

"You can't handle one of those," Cat called back, as if she was working in a loud sandwich shop. "Besides, you're all out of habanero peppers and Fritos. I'll make you a super king on rye. Nobody ever toasts rye."

"Sounds great," I said, getting up. The cupboard above the refrigerator was out of their reach. I reached into it and pulled down an unopened dusty jar of Red Savina peppers and wiped the top off with a towel. I handed her the jar. "Just don't put any of that toxic waste near my sandwich," I said.

The sandwich she made for me was a tower of what looked like a slice of every meat and cheese I owned, each separated by some crunchy or juicy vegetable. There were four or five different condiments. I wondered how I was supposed to get my mouth around it. But it was made in record time, as promised.

Becca had already made hers, a more modest affair that she could eat without doing serious harm to her wardrobe. I watched as Cat built her own sandwich, as tall as mine. She opened the jar of peppers, and took a careful sniff. She speared one with a fork, and carried it to the sink to rinse under the tap.

"The trick is mayonnaise," she said, putting a dab of white goo on her hand, and rubbing her hands together before slicing the pepper. "That, or rubber gloves." When the pepper was sliced, she quickly washed her hands in cold water. "The oil in the mayo absorbs the hot, and the vinegar lets it wash off easily." As she spoke, tears began to run down her face. "That's a good pepper," she said, and pushed the slices onto her sandwich.

Pleased with her handiwork, she placed both hands on top of it and pushed down, until the tall sandwich was just small enough to fit into her wide-open mouth. I did the same to mine, and was able to take a bite. The sandwich was quite good.

Cat had tears streaming down her face, and a big grin.

"I think she gets off on it," Becca said. "She'll be high for the next ten minutes. You should look for addictive behavior in *her* DNA."

We finished lunch and cleaned up. Cat could still barely see as we made our way back out to the genetics lab. Becca ran ahead again, and Cat and I had some fun with the soap before getting into fresh paper coveralls. The sequencer had finished while we were eating lunch.

I brought up the results and ran a comparison between Cat's and Becca's mitochondrial DNA. The results were wrong. Just wrong.

"This is really wrong," I said out loud. "They're a perfect match, just like sisters should be. Except for these two regions. These are so totally different that you wouldn't think they were related before the dark ages." I ran the codes through a search. The women were quiet while the machine did correlation analysis.

"Here," I said, when the first region came up on the screen. "This one is found in Japanese people." The other region was found. "This one is from people from central Kenya. It makes no sense unless they were inserted, but there are no SMTV markers, and no signatures."

I studied the areas at the ends of both strange coding regions. In mitochondrial DNA, there are only a small number of patterns found there, promoter regions, inhibitors, and some not quite random leftovers of evolution. I ran a search on what I had found there. We all waited quietly, until the machine reported "No results".

Despite that nearly blank screen, there was only one explanation that made any sense. "These two regions are the ones that were flagged in Becca's mapper reading. Someone took your mother's mitochondrial DNA and swapped those two areas for clean ones."

I ran another search. "I'm checking, but I'll bet those are known to be superior genes. By that I mean better than average, not just repaired to normal. A slightly more efficient metabolism, slightly better endurance, like that of a long-distance runner." The search completed. The second region was part of a commercial coding region from Geneprime. The first one showed up as a longevity marker in population studies.

"Someone is selling one of them, or at least part of it. And the other one looks like it leads to lower levels of oxidative stress. Definitely better than average, both of them."

"Cat's like you?" Becca asked.

I thought about that for a moment. "No, not like me. The rest of the stuff is normal. The only superior stuff is where there was a significant flaw in the original source material. As if someone were fixing a broken part on a car, and reached for the best possible replacement, but left all the other parts in their stock condition. But it's much worse than that. They went out of their way to conceal what they had done. Not signing your work is easy. Illegal, but easy. You just don't do it. But erasing all traces of any markers used in the gene transfer, that's really hard. I don't know how to do that. Why would someone go to all that trouble? Especially for these genes. The problems they cause are really minor, and easily treatable. Why risk jail for that?"

Cat looked pensive. She looked over at Becca, then at me. "So, do we have the same mother, or what?"

"The eggs came from the same woman. Your egg came from Becca's mother. But somehow the mitochondrial DNA also came from someone Japanese, and some African long-distance runner. And all of the mitochondrial DNA, not just some of it. All of the mitochondria in the egg were modified, or were replaced by clones of one modified mitochondrion. That's another puzzle. How did they manage that trick?" I paused. "To answer your question, you have the same mother. Only Cat has three of them. And two are as likely to be male as female."

Cat looked over at me. "So how many mothers do you have?"

"Thousands. And on average, they all have one testicle and one ovary." It took Cat a while to get the joke. Becca was thinking about something else.

"Dad did something to Cat. That's what Mom said. And when Mom had me, she didn't tell Dad, so he couldn't do it to me. That's why they split up. He must have been really mad." She looked up at me. "What is so messed up about my genes that Dad didn't want me to be born?" Tears were streaming down her face.

"We haven't found a single thing wrong with your genes," I said. But tomorrow, I knew, we would have the whole sequence. What would I tell her then? What if it was something really bad? I changed the subject.

"At least now we know what to tell Sam to look for," I said. "Your mother had evidence of illegal genetic modifications, designed by an expert to be undetectable by standard tests. Technology like that would cost a lot of money to create, and there would be no legal buyers for it, or for its products. And it would take a large organization to come up with it. An organization that would kill to protect itself. And your father is mixed up in it somehow."

"You can't tell Sam that! He'll arrest Dad." Cat was very worried.

"We can leave that part out for now," I said. "But we need to contact your father right away. And we need to do it very carefully."

I did not mention that I had people following her father already. "I have some people in that area that can be discreet. I'll have them get a message to him. I know what I want to say. You two think about what you want to say, and we'll get the message there."

I also didn't say that if Jonathan Worthington were arrested on genetics charges, Sam would not be able to protect him from the resources available to the people who killed Roland Drake.

§

Chapter Eleven

Back in the house, I started making calls, still dressed in the paper coveralls from the greenhouse. First was Sarah, my underworked social planner. She was used to doing miracles on short notice. I described my needs, and she asked the important questions. "Experienced, new victims, or a mix?" she said efficiently.

"Experienced, and any guests they might want to invite," I said. "Make sure everyone knows who is invited, and try to make sure everyone has someone they want to meet or talk to."

"Of course, grandma," she said. She ignores me when I tell her how to do her job.

"It's dress-up, my treat for costumes, run a tab anywhere but Etienne's, no limits."

"I'm putting myself on this guest list," Sarah said. "Who are we trying to impress?"

"Someone needs to get her troubles off her mind," I said, and described Becca.

"Boy girl boy girl, or some extras for the guest of honor?"

"Don't you dare," I said. "No games, she's fragile. And I'll be bringing her sister. And Jake will be coming, I'll have him notify you about any guests he brings."

"Family?" she asked, meaning Sam.

"Absolutely not. And don't invite anyone who might bring him as a guest."

"OK, I have the gist. I'll have the list and the venue in half an hour for approval," she said, and her face disappeared from the screen. She knew better than to waste time with pleasantries.

Next, I called Jacob Bennington and informed him I would be bringing some papers for him, and that Sarah was putting together a dress-up party, and that he'd be getting the guest list soon. "Bring a date, but don't expect me to be nice," I said.

"I never do, asshole," he said, grinning. "Besides, she's met you."

"That would be Diane or Susan," I said. "Good choices for this one. Sarah's running a costume tab for guests at all the best places."

"This is a costume party?"

"No, dress-up. Think prom night."

"Susan will be thrilled. And she knows about Diane, so you can't screw that up."

"You take all the fun out of throwing a party," I said, and closed the connection.

I called Sam. He answered in one of the interrogation rooms this time, anticipating a need for privacy. That meant he had something to ask me. I jumped in first. "It's evidence of illegal human germ-line modification, somehow without any signatures or SMTV markers. Probably a tissue sample, most likely a frozen fertilized embryo. Also, probably in a container traceable to the company doing the alterations."

Sam chewed on this for a while. "You talked with Jonathan Worthington? Or did you find Margaret Jackson?"

"No, people are your forte," I said. "This is all machine work. Deep inference, not admissible as evidence."

"Where are the girls?" he asked.

"I'm not at liberty to say," I hedged.

"Catherine bet a week tops. There was a pool going on here at the station, everyone lost. Five days was a record, J.T. Maybe there's hope for you. Let us know where to find them. I can offer protection."

"Protection from what?" I asked.

"We've lost Jonathan Worthington. Looks like he might be headed this way."

"And you think he intends to harm his children?"

"He's mixed up in this, somehow. He went to ground as soon as badges were flashed. You know what he was working on at Fort Detrick?"

"What?" I asked.

"Haven't a clue. Top secret shit at a military lab. But they work with genetics."

"Hell Sam, everybody works with genetics these days. It's the easiest way to make anything. Code it up and have some bugs crank it out in a brewery."

"Like binary nerve agents?" Sam said.

"Actually, no. That would be easier using conventional chemistry. A geneticist would make a protein toxin."

"I'll keep that in mind. If you see the girls, tell them to call me."

"They're grown women, Sam."

"All you cradle robbers say that." The screen went blank.

A list of people flashed up on the screen. Sarah hates me. All of the people on the list had different reasons for hating me. That's what Sarah calls "experienced". To know me is to love me. Good thing I have lots of money.

Downstairs, Cat and Becca were still trying to agree on what to say to their father. I told them what Sam had said.

"And," I said, "we'll be meeting the courier at a party tonight, so we'll be getting you two dressed up again. But you'll need new outfits. This is less formal, but still fancy dress. We have an appointment at Etienne's, if that's all right with you."

Becca cheered up a bit, and I got a conspiratorial glance from Cat, letting me know she was only going along with this to help her sister feel better. I didn't buy it for a second. She liked looking good and standing next to me in front of people.

They were both used to phones and video, or texting short messages to friends, so it was difficult for them, writing a message by hand on paper, where what they had to say was complicated. But paper is not traceable like electronic communications, so we all sat at the table with paper and pen. I wrote out my short message, and folded the page in half.

They decided to tell him as little as possible, and to try to make it look like they knew nothing, and were not about to learn anything. "Hi Dad. Mom sent us some weird note and said to come right away, but she's not here. We're fine, we'll be back before finals. Love ya. Cat & Bec."

They folded the note in half like I had done, and handed it to me. I placed it in the leather courier bag and locked it.

Sarah had called Grace at Etienne's, and she had picked out several items for both Cat and Becca, and we spent a lot of time there.

Everyone knew I preferred them in nothing at all, and no one asked my opinion. We were fashionably late to the party.

Sarah had booked a banquet hall, and hired a theater group to stage a mystery as we ate catered courses at seats with name tags by each plate. There were dark corners with drinks and canapés where people could stand and talk about the other guests. Sarah met us at the door.

"You must be the misses Worthington," she said to Becca and Cat. "Fabulous outfits, absolutely perfect for this evening's entertainment. We'll be in groups of six to solve the mystery, the name tags are all color coded so you know who is in your group."

Our group was the three of us, Jacob, Susan, and a young man I did not know. The name card at his plate said James Dupree, so I knew him to be Sarah's guest. He was much too young to be her date, so I assumed Sarah was playing games with Becca, against my instructions. People do that to me. They never learn.

I explained my suspicions to Becca, and told her to have fun with it if she liked, or ignore him and just talk to anyone she liked. I called Cat over, and was giving a rundown of the guest list to both of them, so they would know who interested them and perhaps how to start a conversation, when Jacob and Susan walked over to us.

"Hello, asshole," Susan said, smiling. "Who invited you to this party?" She stepped close and kissed me on the cheek. She was wearing a low-cut scarlet dress with a wide full skirt, the blouse fastened between her breasts with a large ruby broach. She stepped back and gestured at the dress. "You like this?" she asked, and spun around so the dress belled out. "It cost a fortune."

It was obvious that the dress had no place for a brassiere, and she curtsied low to prove that to me, the heavy broach opening up the view to show two perfect breasts, nipples dark against white flesh.

Jacob stepped up to me, and in a soft conspiratorial voice, said "You created this monster yourself you know."

"I only told her the truth," I said.

"In your own 'sock full of lead shot' way," he said.

Becca and Susan were off admiring each other's clothing. Cat came up to join us.

"What are you two whispering about?" she asked.

"Something very rude this man once said to my secretary," Jacob offered.

"Rude is a matter of perception. I stated the truth, and she decided to be offended."

Jacob turned to Cat. "He said she dressed like a frump, and that if she ever wanted to get in my bed, she should stop wasting a perfect set of tits and undo a button or two."

Cat looked over at Susan. She seemed to be thinking for a moment. "Did she get in your bed?" she asked, innocently.

Jacob gave a weak shrug and a nod.

"Then I guess it worked," she said, moving closer to me, and stealthily squeezing my hand.

My other hand held the courier's pouch. I handed it to Jacob. "Sam says they've lost Jonathan Worthington," I said.

"He's in town. At the Carlton, under the name James Watson."

"How original. He can keep the monogrammed underwear. Has he contacted any old friends?" I asked.

"He went by his ex-wife's place," Jacob said, looking over at Cat. "He made the plain clothes car though, and didn't hang around."

"She had let him know where she lived." I stated.

"Looks like it. He went straight there. He paid cash for a bus ticket in Fredericks, spent three days sleeping on a bus seat, then took city transportation to the nearest stop. Left no electronic records. He knows what he's up against."

"Someone is doing germ-line genetic modifications in humans, and deleting all traces of it. That takes a very high level of skill and knowledge, some impressive computing resources, access to patented genetic intellectual property, human eggs, in-vitro fertilization equipment and skills, and the ability to remove mitochondria from the egg without killing it, and replace the mitochondria with altered versions without leaving any of the originals around. There's no published research on that last trick. And they like to kill people with military binary nerve agents. We're not looking for one guy. We're looking for a well funded organization, with front businesses that can order this kind of equipment without raising eyebrows."

Jacob took all this in. "I assume you have your own searches running on all those avenues."

"No results yet. I asked for very high confidence, and no traceable searches. If they see someone snooping around, the game suddenly gets very dangerous."

Jacob nodded. "My people are being very careful not to be noticed. No electronic tracking, never the same tail twice. But the target is carrying a signed rhinovirus, that makes it easier."

"Yours or theirs?" I asked.

"Ours. No other infections found. So even if these guys are using something unsigned, they haven't gotten to Worthington."

Cat looked up at me. "They gave him a cold?"

I explained. "It's an easy way to track someone. Snot gets every-where, that's how colds spread. Tag the virus with a signature, and you can track someone. They leave a little bit on every doorknob, every taxi, every sidewalk, every wall and window."

"That's just disgusting."

"But highly effective," Jacob said.

The first course was being served, and we all took our places. Becca was having a lively conversation with James Dupree, involving a lot of giggling. I leaned over the table and spoke to him.

"So, your mother is a big fan of Milne?" I asked. "Did she go for the full five middle names?"

He stopped gazing at Becca and looked up at me. He considered carefully what he wanted to say.

"Sarah already warned me about you," he said, smiling. "But I as-sume that won't help me a bit."

"Never does," I said, smiling back. "Enjoy the evening."

Sarah had placed me between Cat and Becca, and across from Su-san, who was flanked by Jacob and young Dupree. Susan seemed to enjoy flexing her cleavage and making sure her nipples were erect by occasionally rubbing them against the edge of the table. I made a point of making sure she knew I noticed. Her right hand stayed in Jacob's lap.

There was a loud gunshot from the doorway to the cloakroom, and the hat check girl ran out into the room, screaming. "Someone shot

Mr. Conrad!" she said, excitedly. The evening's entertainment had begun.

As the courses were served, the actors brought out a police inspector, and a succession of witnesses, and gradually the mystery fleshed out. There were cards and pencils by each plate for noting key clues and motives, and before dessert was brought out, each group had to decide who had murdered Mr. Conrad, and why.

It was clear who was supposed to be the killer, and which were the distractors, but theater groups are allowed to cheat and pick anyone. I had to figure out if Sarah had rigged one table to win or lose, and what I wanted to do about it. The actual game was uninteresting. Sarah's game, if she was playing one, was more of a challenge. She knows I am extremely competitive, but not at trivial matters. If she wanted to challenge me, she would have to play for stakes worth winning. That meant Dupree and Becca would be involved.

If our table was targeted, either we would win the game, or be the only table not to win. I scanned my memory of the other tables, and how they had reacted to the various clues. They would all pick the obvious killer. If Sarah was not playing games, this was a very easy mystery to solve, and all the tables would solve it. That may actually be the intention.

Jacob and Susan would both have given accidental hints if they had been in on any deception. It is very difficult to play poker with me. Dupree had already admitted to being part of Sarah's scheming, and so had a perfect reason for appearing conspiratorial. If he was a plant, he could not throw the game all by himself. That meant that winning or losing was not relevant. What was going to matter was my interaction with Dupree, and how that affected Becca. I leaned towards Becca, and whispered softly.

"You seem to have him just where you want him," I said.

She whispered back. "Call your friend the shrink. But if that doesn't work, I may need someone disposable in a hurry."

Whatever game Sarah wanted to play; it was not going to work. Becca was inoculated, and nothing this night threw at her was going to bother her. Thus, there were no stakes worth playing for, and I could stop second guessing everything.

"So," I said to the table, "Is it Colonel Mustard in the Library with a Candlestick?"

Dupree looked up. Yes, Sarah was playing games. "I think it was the hat check girl," he said, ignoring the consensus that it was the detective.

"That's actually brilliant," I said. "I think the rest of the tables are going for the detective. If we all go for him, then the whole game gets pretty boring. But if we go for someone unlikely, such as the hat check girl, then we have a one in five chance of winning, assuming the game is rigged and the detective is meant to be obvious." I looked around at the others at the table. "What do you say we go for it?"

No one wanted to disagree with me. Of course. We voted for the hat check girl.

"Now we need a reason," Jacob said. "Why do we think it was the hat check girl?"

We all looked at one another. Becca spoke. "Because she's not wearing any underwear."

Jacob looked up. "She's not wearing any underwear?"

Becca said "Who would wear underwear to a party like this?" She looked over at Susan. "Right?"

Susan giggled. "Absolutely."

Becca looked cross at Dupree. "But mostly because I want to hear Jim announce that to the whole room."

We all laughed and Dupree wrote the reason on the card.

Sarah had met her match in Becca.

Of course, in the end, it was the detective. Becca was consoling Dupree when dessert arrived, and she had him order for her.

As the party was breaking up, Becca and Dupree were whispering in a quiet corner alone. Cat, Jacob, Susan, and I were chatting when Sarah approached me.

"You asshole," she said. "You let me win!"

I looked over at Becca and Dupree. "No, " I said. "She did."

Cat squeezed my hand again. We said goodbyes to Jacob and Susan, and called to Becca that the valet had brought the car.

When we got home, I quickly went upstairs alone, and booked an emergency appointment with Doctor Clay Garret, the best psychiatrist on the west coast. I have all four of them on retainer. He would move his calendar around to fit us in.

§

Chapter Twelve

The house woke me before dawn. I dressed quickly, and quietly left for the greenhouse. I wanted to get as much analysis done as I could on the sequence data before having to explain anything to Cat and Becca. Not only was I very eager to learn what was hidden there, but I knew that whatever I found would have to be explained in just the right way. And for that I wanted a head start.

Certain that I would find nasty surprises there, I pulled up Becca's results first. I did a scan for known fatal genetic disorders. A handful showed up. Hinshaw Barnes was not there. So much for her main fear. She had won that coin toss. The others were the normal problems associated with aging. All were treatable with diet, exercise, or drug interventions.

The list of harmful disorders was much longer. Still, the number and severity of the problems fell well within the normal range. Light related depression, hormonal mood swings, reduced ability to detect bitter tastes. In addition to the mitochondrial risk markers, she had three nuclear DNA risk markers. She might be more likely than normal to take up hobbies like race car driving or hang gliding. There were also problems in the dopamine and norepinephrine transport mechanisms associated with depression and drug addiction, and some irregularities in serotonin receptor proteins. All treatable.

Basically, there was nothing wrong with Becca. Genetically.

I kept looking. The list of known genetic disorders is long, and most people seem to have at least a third of them. I started some searches on problems caused by combinations of the markers on the list. That would take a while.

It began to look like if there was any mystery here, it was not in Becca's DNA. But I needed to be thorough, so I continued analyzing even the smallest of problems. Certain antibiotics might make her nauseous. She probably sneezed when she walked from a dark room into the sunlight. I was aware that I was deliberately putting off looking at Cat's data. It was getting late. They were probably up already.

I pulled up Cat's results. The scan for fatal disorders showed none. The scan for known harmful disorders was smaller than mine. Not a single one had been discovered before Cat was born.

The next step was much more complicated. I dictated a program to search for each of the items on Becca's list, and find the best replacement for that section of DNA that was known at the estimated time of Cat's conception, and compare that to what was found at that location in Cat's results.

The search took time, but as each one came up on the screen, my suspicions were confirmed. There were exceptions. Sometimes a second or third best replacement had been used. When I researched those, it usually came up that the choices were so close that it would not matter. In some of the cases the benefits of the best selection had not been known at the time of her conception. But in each case, someone had replaced a defective region from Becca's DNA with the best replacement they had.

I expanded the search. Instead of using Becca's list, I used the list of all known disorders. Some more replacements started showing up in the results.

It was one thing to erase all signs of the markers that indicate a replacement had been done. But anyone looking at these results would immediately know that this DNA had been tampered with. With all the elaborate precautions being taken not to get caught, this one glaring exception made no sense. Remove a spot or two from a Dalmatian and no one would notice. Remove them all, and the fire department would have a plain white dog that anyone could see was not a Dalmatian.

I could hear water running in the shower. I was about to have company.

I started working on another program. No one can completely erase their tracks in a data stream, and DNA was a data stream like any other. Statistical methods are available for finding embezzlers and tax cheats, and the same tricks could be used here. Now that I had a sample of their work, I should be able to find traces of it elsewhere. Not just which regions were replaced, but subtle patterns in the nearby base sequences, promoters, inhibitors, frequencies of occurrence of pairs of regions taken together — I could build an inference search that would find other people who had been tampered with. If I had samples of their DNA.

Cat and Becca had showered in together.

"Thought we'd find you here," Becca said. "We waited hours for you to come down for breakfast or a workout. A note would have been nice, asshole."

Cat was more understanding. "What did you find out?"

I had decided to stick to what I had found in Cat's results first. I showed them the list of all known defects found in the population, and the list of those that were found in Cat. I pointed out that the ones found in Cat had only been discovered after she had been conceived.

"But it's not just that. Each one was replaced by the best-known substitute at the time. Each one is substantially above normal. Better cognitive function, better physical performance, better immune response, less autoimmune sensitivity, less carcinogenic tendency, on down the list, it's all improvement. Some of the most expensive patented gene therapies were used, I'm sure without payment."

Becca looked over at me. "She's like you."

"No," I said, "Not like me at all. My father used an entirely different method. He selected for success across a wide range of occupations. He used tens of thousands of sequence templates, and years of computer time. Only when he had come up with the best total sequence he could find using those criteria did he hand-edit a few genes, buying some special ones, like longevity, that don't correlate with his original criteria. I was designed from the ground up to be successful, even if that meant having severe flaws in personality or socialization."

I looked over at Cat. "Cat was designed to be flawless. Not the best — most of her genome was untouched, unimproved. But each known flaw was replaced by the best code available at the time. But only the flaws, not the perfectly adequate genes that just happened not to be optimal."

No one spoke for a while. Becca squirmed on the stool. "What did you find out about the person in the room who wasn't born according to some genius master plan."

I spoke carefully, trying to carve just the right path through her heart. Sometimes you have to cut deep, and get it over with.

"You're a mess. A pharmacist's dream. Not as much of a mess as most people, but there's plenty here to make you want to keep your health insurance premiums paid up. You're going to need to watch your cholesterol levels, your blood pressure, your triglycerides. You have a tendency towards type II diabetes, so you should watch your weight as you get older. You will get presbyopia probably around age 39, so you'll need reading glasses or a flexible lens replacement. You should be careful not to get too much blue light after sundown in the wintertime, or else take a good antidepressant. I'm sure all of this is in your medical records. Any blood test would be on record there. Your doctors should be giving you good advice."

"That's it?" she asked.

"Oh, it goes on for pages and pages. You could be in here reading for days. Like I said, you're normal."

Becca and Cat both looked suspicious. They must have read something in my voice, or known something else was coming.

"And one more thing," I said. "No sign of Hinshaw Barnes."

Becca stood up quickly, a look of hurt and hatred in her eyes. She aimed her fist at my face. From years of practice, I let the hard knuckles slam into my broken nose and knock me off my stool. She ran for the door to the showers. "You asshole!" she shouted. "You *knew* I didn't want to know!" The she was through the door, slamming it shut behind her.

Cat watched as I picked myself up, and held my bleeding nose to the paper sleeve of my coverall. "Why did you do that?" she asked, eyes narrowed.

"She knew I was an asshole when she walked in," I said.

"You knew exactly what you were doing. You knew what she wanted. Why couldn't you just say what she wanted to hear and leave it at that?"

I looked at Cat through eyes that watered from the pain of my nose alone. "I don't tell people what they want to hear," I told her. "I tell people what they need to know."

She turned and walked to the door. I followed, holding my head up to stop the bleeding. She stepped out of the greenhouse onto the lawn, and I stepped out after her, looking up at the sky. Becca's fist caught me in the solar plexus, and I went down again, legs fold-ing beneath me, my diaphragm spasming, unable to draw a breath.

"Last night," she shouted, "Jimmy told me that half the people in the room had earned the right to call you 'asshole'. He said it like it was some kind of club, some initiation or something. He was actually looking forward to you treating him badly, like it would make him special. What the hell is wrong with you? Why do you treat people like that? Why do you go out of your way to be a com-plete asshole? I thought it was just the Trip reaction making me hate you, but no, it's you. It's not me who's fucked up, it's you. I hate you!"

She ran off towards the house, sobbing. I watched her run, and said, loudly enough for Cat to hear, "Join the club."

Cat held out her hand. "Get up asshole," she said. "She has a shrink appointment in an hour and your breakfast is stone cold. She made you a special omelet, and you're going to eat every last bite."

§

Chapter Thirteen

The ride to the Clay Garret's office was quiet. Two hours of quiet, since his office was north of the bay and traffic was no better than normal for this time of day. Cat refused to sit up front with me, and joined Becca in the back. Becca had stopped crying, and was curled up with her knees under her chin in a sullen funk. No one spoke for the whole trip.

Clay Garret's offices were a sprawling park-like set of low buildings poured like honey over the cliffs above the low rumble of the Pacific Ocean's attempts to reclaim the sandstone that used to be an ocean bottom in the Late Cretaceous. Pines shaded slate paths leading between buildings, and flowering groundcover melted over low walls and across to the cliffs. A light fog was clearing, and the Pacific stretched out past kelp and whitecaps to the horizon.

The setting was quiet and beautiful, and as Cat and Becca left the car, I could see that both of them were transfixed by the view and the peaceful sounds of surf and blue jays. As I led them to the main office over a bridge above the koi pond, they watched squirrels jump from tree to tree, and seagulls ride the ridge lift over the cliffs.

I held the glass door open, and the women entered ahead of me.

The lobby got very quiet as the door closed, and we walked through the large carpeted lobby to the receptionist's desk. She looked up at me.

"Hey asshole, long time no see," she said, flashing a large diamond ring on her left hand as if daring me not to notice. "You missed the wedding."

"Consider that a gift to your guests," I said. "Is Clay ready for us?"

"He's cleared his afternoon. He's in the solarium, if you want to just charge in." She waved down the hallway.

As we passed her desk, Becca caught her eye. "I think I'm going to start calling him butthead, just to be different."

"I tried dickwad for a few weeks," came the answer. "Seemed to make *me* feel good."

The solarium was a large glass-walled room half buried in the sloping rocks of the cliffside, and half cantilevered over the carpet of flowers leading to the edge of the cliff. The sun was just starting to warm the room through the glass ceiling, on which lay scattered pine needles that must drive the cleaning staff crazy. The thick off-white carpet matched the long couches facing the ocean. Clay himself was sitting at one end of a couch, reading notes on a computer screen. The screen blanked as we came in, and Clay Garret stood up.

He was tall, elegantly dressed down to large sapphire cuff links on a freshly pressed lavender dress shirt open at the collar. He had thick straight hair pulled back in a short pony tail, gray and white mixed with shiny black. He looked like a model for a men's clothing business, or a Hollywood lawyer. His smile was genuine and warm, but directed at the women.

"Clay Garret," he said, extending a hand towards them as he walked up. "Which of you is Rebecca Worthington?" The last bit was a formality, as he was already walking up to Becca, who took his offered hand. He gave her hand a brief polite squeeze and let go.

"I normally deal with clients one-on-one, but if you'd like to keep your support group with you, that is fine with me," he said.

"No, actually I think I'd rather be private," Becca said, looking around the room, not at anyone in it.

"Very well then. Doctor Wright," he said, turning to me, "Perhaps you and Catrina can find something to do in town, or walk around the grounds. Rosalind will call you when we're done here, but Rebecca may want to have the rest of the afternoon, and the blood tests will take an hour at least anyway."

Becca looked up at him. "Blood tests?"

"To see how you metabolize the medication you're on. I trust you brought a sample with you? We'll want to analyze it. That way we can custom tailor a treatment." Becca nodded.

He waved at the door and smiled at Cat and me. That smile was formal, not warm or genuine. We left the room, Cat looking back at Becca, who was staring out at the ocean.

We walked past Rosalind at the front desk without a word, and I held the door for Cat. The ocean breeze and the low roar of the surf were a noted contrast to the quiet of the offices.

"There's no one else around here," Cat said, noting the empty parking lot. "This place is huge, and they're just the two of them here?"

"His practice does very well, and he enjoys reminding people of that," I said. "But if you're trying to forget your troubles, you could do worse than come to a place like this."

We walked on the slate path under the pines. A sunny manicured lawn stretched out on the north side of the buildings.

"Sam calls you J.T.," Cat said. "What's the T. for?"

"Thomas," I said.

"Jack Thomas Wright," she said. "I've known you for a week now. The puzzle pieces are starting to fit together. You've been extremely nice, an outrageously generous host. When am I going to get my 'asshole moment'?"

I kicked at a pine cone on the walk. "What makes you think you need one?" I asked.

"Don't I get to be part of the club?"

I watched her as she walked. "Are you feeling left out?"

"If you don't want to answer the question, then don't answer. That's all right. I'll just ask a different question."

"Go ahead, ask anything you like," I said.

"I've been flirting with you for days now. How come you haven't jumped my bones yet?"

I kicked the pine cone again. "Social skills were never one of my strong points."

"What were you doing cruising around the liquor store at three in the morning?"

"I was looking to get laid," I said.

"And you found Becca. You must be the luckiest guy on the planet. So how come you never get lucky? She would have done anything for you that night, you know. Anything and everything."

"I know."

"But that wasn't what you were looking for," Cat said quietly.

"It's not what she needed," I said.

"That sounds like the asshole we all know and love. What about what *you* needed?"

"If I could figure out what I needed, I'd be a happier man."

"Maybe you just need to get laid."

"What would Becca say?"

"She's been giving me flirting tips all week. She's been waiting for days to hear the bed banging the wall."

"And what if that doesn't fix all my problems?" I asked.

She put her arm around my waist and drew me closer. "Then I guess we'll just have to keep trying," she said.

We walked that way in silence for a while. Getting the rhythm right took a second or two, but after that it seemed surprisingly natural. I put my arm around her shoulder.

"So why did you do that to Becca?" she asked quietly, resting her head against me. "You know how important it was to her not to get tested, not to know."

"It's one thing not to want to be know you will die young. It is another to be upset when someone tells you that you won't. That indicates how much of her self-image and personality have been shaped by this one issue. Now she has a future to plan for, and that's a responsibility she has been able to avoid so far. The future is a scary thing. But she needed to have a future she could look forward to, in order to sort out her current problems."

"I think you really need to work on your delivery," she said.

"On the contrary. This is the way that works best, in all my tests over many years. You just have to accept that people will hate you for it, and do it anyway."

"So, besides arrogance, what other personality flaws come with a genome built for success?"

"Overbearing competitiveness, even when no one else is compet-ing, for one thing. A drive to do everything better than anyone else, faster than anyone else, sooner than anyone else. I made more money than my father ever did, at a much younger age. I collected advanced degrees at a younger age than anyone, more of them than anyone. It has taken years of work to tame that drive, with the help of people like Clay Garret, so it didn't consume me. But I still can't tolerate people who hold themselves back because of fear or laziness or ignorance. People who walk on the fence between success and mediocrity without ever taking that one easy step, those people I push over, so they fall on the success side. I have all the risk-taking genes, all the optimist genes, so everything that comes my way looks like an opportunity. When people can't see things the way I do, I shove them off the fence."

"You're forgetting some other personality traits of successful people."

"Oh yes. Ruthlessness. I have that in buckets. Pride. Stubbornness. A sense of entitlement. A chip glued to my shoulder. Impatience. Selfishness."

"I was thinking of charisma, compassion, generosity, vision, honesty. And pride is not the deadly sin they would have you believe it is. It's what makes us want to do something well."

"Your opinion doesn't count. You have the same damn optimist genes."

She was quiet for a while. "I think it's your opinion that counts," she said. "Maybe you should work on that pride a little more."

"Or I could chuck the whole thing and try to develop a sense of humor."

The roads by the sea twist with the coast, but they also rise and fall. The path ended at the road, and the road went steeply down to the mouth of the river. The small tourist town that had grown up where the river met the sea was festooned with colorful flags, kites, and windsocks to attract the attention of vacationing motorists.

Small sailboats were racing inside the sandbar breakwater, and the sea breeze was blowing Cat's hair away from her face. I liked the smile I saw there, and the childlike excitement of seeing new things.

In town we stopped for ice cream. Then we rented a small sailboat, and I taught her how to sail. She loved the sense of speed she could get when the wind was right and the boat heeled over, the water bubbling and hissing against the thin hull. We were wind burned and sun burned when we brought the boat back, and we had just opened a couple of cold root beers when Cat's new phone called attention to itself in her pants pocket. Becca was done with her session.

The hike back up the hill gradually became a race. I stayed a meter ahead of Cat as she picked up speed, until finally she was sprinting flat out up the steep hill. She kept up the pace, occasionally almost closing the distance between us before I lengthened my stride. At the top of the hill, I tagged the pine that marked the beginning of the path, and slowed to a walk. Cat slowed to walk beside me, chest heaving, a sheen of fine sweat covering her face and neck.

"You were holding back," she said.

"I like to watch you run," I replied. I raised my arms to the cool breeze to dry the sweat from my shirt.

A few minutes later, we had mostly caught our breath, and somewhat dried out, and we entered the building. Rosalind was sitting behind her desk, and Becca and Garret were standing next to it, chatting with her. We handed our empty root beer bottles to Rosalind, and Cat turned to Becca.

"How'd things go?"

"Ok, I guess," Becca said, fingering the gauze and tape on her inner elbow where the blood had been taken. "I got some pills that should help, and this one killer pill I'm supposed to take only in a dire emergency, because you can only take it once in your whole life." She held out a small stainless steel pill container on a steel cable around her neck, like that used to hang heavy pictures in a museum. "There's just one big red pill in there, in case things get really bad."

Garret looked up at me. "Manheim protocol," he said. I nodded, a serious look on my face.

"I got pills for the cramps and the nausea, but he says I'll still go through the shakes and chills, and I'll feel really awful, just like in the hospital. But once I'm past that, this other set of pills will make it so I don't crave anymore." She held out a blister pack of pills, each marked with a date and time to be taken. "You take a bunch at first, and then taper them off."

Cat looked worried. "You were a mess in the hospital," she reminded Becca.

"I know. But I think I can do it this time. We had a long talk about everything. I really want to do this."

"Let me know if I can help," Cat said.

"Oh, you're in the plan, definitely. Even butthead's in the plan, whether he likes it or not."

"I'm hoping I can be of some help, somehow," I said.

We walked back out to the car. This time, Cat took the front seat, and Becca stretched out sideways in the back. The back seat shifted shape to conform to her position, and extruded a pillow. We watched the coastal scenery flow by in silence for a long time, then the car finally found a straight road and headed inland.

"I think I've figured out why you never got your face fixed," Becca said sleepily.

I didn't answer.

"Why fix it when you're just going to make someone break it again?" she concluded.

I brought my hand up to my nose. "I think you may actually have straightened it out a bit," I said.

"Good. A few more punches and you'll be good as new. I'll help out when you least expect it," she said, and then pretended to go to sleep.

The drugs she had been given were speeding the onset of her withdrawal. She was shaking by the time we got home, and Cat and I helped her upstairs and into bed. It was already late, but neither Cat nor I wanted to leave her bedside. Cat stroked her sister and tried to ease the trembling. After an hour or so of this, Becca looked up at her sister.

"If you two insist on hanging around all night, get the hell under the covers and keep me warm."

Cat removed her clothes and climbed under the covers, snuggling up close to her sister. "You too, butthead," Becca said to me, "I told you that you were part of the plan."

I left my clothes on the floor and crawled into bed on Becca's other side. She turned towards me and pressed herself against my back, an arm around my waist, her whole body shaking. Cat snuggled behind her the same way. "We have a Becca sandwich," she said, and reached a hand across her sister to place it on my hip.

None of us got much sleep. When Becca wasn't shaking, she curled up in a fetal position and moaned. Cat and I took turns wiping the sweat from her body with damp towels at these times, before the chills returned. The pills for the cramping and nausea were not completely effective, and at times we had to rub knots out of her muscles. Bouts of shallow hyperventilation alternated with dry heaves, and her temperature swung from fever to deathly cold three times during the night.

By late morning, things were worse for Becca, although Cat managed to get a half hour of sleep just before eleven. By noon, Becca's temperature had dropped so low I ran a hot bath in the huge tub, and Cat and I carried her in, and slipped into the hot water on either side of her. Through all of this she gripped the waterproof steel canister on her cable necklace as if her life depended on it. But she did not open it and take the pill. She was determined to use that only as a very last resort, when she no longer had the strength to resist.

With her temperature once more that of the living, we stood her up and turned on the blast of hot air to dry us all off. I carried her back to the bed, and Cat and I got in beside her again. It was three in the afternoon when both of them finally fell asleep. It was dark when I awoke. Becca was whimpering, tears falling onto my arm.

"It hurts, it really hurts. My belly, my head, my muscles, my eyes, my fucking tits even hurt."

"We can't help you there. All of the pain relievers affect the same systems that you're trying to reset."

"Except one," she said, holding out her fist, still tightly holding the can at the end of the cable around her neck.

"That's your decision," I said gently.

"I don't dare. What if I can't go through the whole week? What if I have to do this all over again after I fuck up? I need to keep this just in case. I only get one shot at it."

I kissed her on the forehead. She put her head down on my shoulder and pulled me against her tightly. After a few minutes, her grip relaxed, and she fell back to sleep.

It was daylight when I awoke to the smell of toast and scrambled eggs. Cat and Becca were both awake, sitting up in bed. Becca was slowly nursing a cup of broth. Cat was crunching loudly on a piece of toast, the remains of her plate of eggs wiped clean. A plate of eggs, toast, and a glass of orange juice were waiting for me on the bedside table. I was starving. I also needed to pee badly, and had a stiff erection that the sight of the two naked women in the bed were not helping to prevent. I stood up to go to the bathroom. Becca eyed my predicament. "Somebody woke up happy," she said, giving Cat a weak grin.

I took a shower and was much more relaxed when I came back to bed, putting my plate of cold eggs on my lap. "How are you doing?" I asked Becca.

"I feel like shit," she said. "I'm still cribbing too, and all I can think about is that tiny little pill in my purse."

"He let you keep those?" Cat asked, surprised.

"He said it was important. Part of the process. I can give in anytime, go back to what I was. Or I can decide that I'm in charge for now. And for now, I am."

"When do you take the pills that stop the cravings?" Cat asked.

"What day is it?" Becca asked. The house answered. "Shit," she said, reaching up on the headboard for the blister packed pills. She read the date and time for the first pill. "Noon today. Think I can start an hour early?"

"Let's try it by the book," I suggested. "But in the end, it's all up to you."

"I can hang out for another hour. I think the headache is from dehydration. The whole bed is drenched in sweat."

Since we were all awake, I took the house out of privacy mode. Immediately there were two priority message alerts, one from Sam, and one from Jacob. I brought Sam's up first.

"Hey J.T., do you think you can find the Worthington girls again? Jonathan Worthington ordered a gun the day after the girls left home. They have a 10-day waiting period in Maryland for handguns, and the day the gun was in his hands is the day he disappeared. His co-workers say he was on shaky ground mentally. We're still looking for his ex-wife, who we think may be in danger, and the girls may also be potential targets."

"He's gonna do it," Becca said.

"He said he would, before the meds became totally useless," Cat said.

"Just for the record, are we talking about suicide?" I asked.

"He said he didn't want to go out like his father. When the time came, he said he'd put a gun to his head before he lost the ability to know what a gun was," Cat explained.

"Why didn't he just stay home? God, it's half the reason we left home, so we didn't have to be part of that. Now he shows up here. Can't he just leave us alone?" Becca was starting to sweat again.

"Is there any chance he's a danger to you or your mother? I can tell Sam where he is, and the police could pick him up and put him on a suicide watch," I said.

"This isn't like that. He's not some despondent depressive you want to talk out of it. This is a rational decision that we all agreed on. Life expectancy for Hinshaw Barnes is 48 years old. His meds have given him another two years, but they can't stop the mental decay. He's choosing the time and manner of his death. And apparently the place. We said our goodbyes already. Maybe he's here to say goodbye to Mom." Cat had rehearsed this speech, at least to herself.

"So, when we find your mother, we can arrange for them to meet at d'Artagnan's. He won't be able to get a gun past the security there. After that, we leave them alone," I said. "In the meantime, I'll let Sam know you got his message. But I won't mention the suicide — Sam would have to intervene."

I brought up Jacob's message.

"Hi Jack. We're starting to get multiple hits on the rhinovirus, so we have a partial list of people he's been in close contact with. But that also means he's getting harder to track with sniffers, so we've had to go back to tailing him. We're preparing a cocktail of three more tags, so we'll know it's him for sure. The odds of passing all three to someone else are pretty slim. Something else you should know. We have compiled a list of his contacts in the local area, from about 24 years ago. And a surprising number of them are no longer among the living. One natural causes, seven accidents, out of fifteen so far. It ain't healthy to be this guy's friend."

"Interesting," I said. I left a return message. No need for a real-time chat. "Send me the list, and what data you have on them, I'll set up an inference search to see what connections pop up. And send the same list to Sam."

Cat looked over at me. "What's to stop Dad from just going into a drug store and getting a cold pill?"

"The broad-spectrum antivirals sold over the counter are designed to treat the viruses found in the local environment. They are tailored to those viruses. The ones Jake is using are not local to any area, they're entirely synthetic. And since they're entirely harmless and produce no symptoms, they're legal under the tag laws for epidemiology research. He's not sneezing and coughing, but everyone touches their eyes and nose, and the virus spreads easily. If it spread too easily though, it would not be useful to us."

"So, he doesn't really have a cold," Becca said.

"A very mild one," I said. "He'll have a sniffle or two."

The house announced that Jacob had delivered the list of Jonathan Worthington's local contacts.

"I'm going upstairs to set up some programming. You're welcome to join me if you like."

"I'm going back to sleep," Becca said. "Probably until next week."

"I'll tag along," Cat said.

We went upstairs. The search for commonalities in the short list did not take long to set up, but I added some safeguards against anyone potentially watching for such a search, and added a few questions the inference engine might not have come up with on its own, and then launched the search. Some results appeared immediately. Many of the people on the list had worked with Jonathan Worthington, or worked at places he had once worked, or had similar jobs. The program rearranged the list into three parts, with people in each part having something in common, such as knowing one another, or knowing some other individual. The smallest of the lists were people who knew Margaret Jackson. The program, like most of my inference searches, would continue running in the background, gradually coming to conclusions based on the data it found, and coming up with new searches on its own, based on its inferences.

The screen showed a number of items awaiting my attention on other matters. The search for connections between Roland Drake, genetic engineering, and nerve agents was stalled. This usually in-dicated that the search was too tightly constrained. I rewrote the query, removing the connection between genetics and nerve agents. The people with access to nerve agents apparently had ei-ther no connections to genetics, or no connections to Drake, and the latter seemed much less likely, given the method of his death.

This search, being broader, brought up results right away. It would be up to me to try to see what those results had in common, and to then write a better query. Some things computers were good at, but I was particularly good at finding subtle patterns in large search spaces with little information. I let the back of my mind work on the list of results and focused my attention on the economic data in the next message.

Cat was reading ahead. "There's something about me," she said, pointing to a line that had her name and a dollar amount.

I selected the item. "Income from financial derivatives transac-tions." I turned to Cat. "The house needs to know where to put your money."

"What money?" she asked.

"You placed two puts and a call with the guest budget. The trans-actions have finalized. Where would you like the money to go?"

"How much money are we talking about?" she asked.

I pointed to the number in the heading.

She took it in slowly. "How much of that was the guest budget?"

"About a third," I said, touching the screen. An analysis came up, and I pointed to the number 3.09.

"Christ on a pogo stick," she said softly. "You let your guests spend half a million dollars on clothes and pizza?"

"Not really. I set up a perfectly reasonable amount in the account about 12 years ago, and had it invested in my hedge fund. I've done particularly well with the fund over the last 12 years, and you are the first visitors to actually use any of it."

"So, I just made over a million bucks in what, four days? And you do that all the time?"

"Oh, no, not at all," I said. "A lot of my hunches are wrong, and when I'm wrong, I usually lose a lot more money than that. If this were easy, everyone would be doing it, and there would be no money to make. You just lucked out."

"Just lucked out," she said softly. "What do I do now?"

"My advice for someone in your place?" I asked. "First, pay off all your debts. Student loans, credit cards, whatever. Then open an account with a broad index fund, and a bond fund, and a cash account for the taxes you owe on this. If there was more, I'd suggest a down payment on some real estate. Buy a house."

"How much are the taxes?" she asked.

"Figure about half of the profits."

"Shit, just when I thought I was rich," she said.

"That still leaves you over a million dollars," I pointed out.

"Half of that goes back into the guest account," she said.

"There's no need for that. If you had lost the money, would you still be planning on paying the account back?"

"I never really thought about it. I had no idea there was so much money there. But it goes back, that's only fair." She looked up at me and grinned. "Besides, I'm still a guest, right?"

"Absolutely," I said.

"Becca's gonna shit."

I turned to the other items on the screen, and resumed working. Cat seemed lost in thought. I finished about twenty minutes later, and turned off the screen. Cat looked up from her reverie, and we started down the stairs.

"I could go to grad school," she said.

"What are you studying?"

"I'll have a double E next semester. But I was thinking genetics, or maybe finance. That seems to have worked out for you. Last week they would have seemed really boring."

"You'll have lots of time to make a decision."

We checked in on Becca, who was asleep, as she had predicted. We were walking to the kitchen when something triggered in my subconscious.

"You and Becca spent the night on the roof of a supermarket," I said to Cat.

"Yeah. Nobody can see you up there, you don't get hassled."

"What gave you that idea?" I asked.

"Something Mom said once. She used to dry out sometimes, before she met Dad. She's been an alky burner for a long time."

I used the screen in the kitchen to call Jacob Bennington. His face came up, the bookcases in his office behind him. "Jake," I said, "Margaret Jackson is probably spending nights on rooftops to avoid detection. Get some aerial shots of the neighborhoods where she lived and worked, and of any areas Jonathan Worthington has been checking out. Look for signs of occupancy, like a sleeping bag, or fast-food trash or something."

Cat spoke up. "Southern comfort bottles, the little flat pint ones."

"I'll get someone on that," Jacob said. The screen went blank. Jacob knew better than to expect small talk from me.

I showed Cat how to bone a chicken. We put the bones in a pressure cooker with a couple quarts of water, and sliced up the meat into bite sized chunks and sautéed them in the fat from the chicken skin. I showed her how to tie herbs in a cheesecloth bag, and we left the meat and the bag alone while the bones cooked into a broth. Since this was going to take a while, I went back upstairs to check on the search results. Cat went to check in on Becca.

It turns out that AC 13 is a difficult binary nerve agent for an amateur to produce. Most of the steps involve proscribed or monitored chemical building blocks, and most of those require specialized equipment or long lead times. It was beginning to sound like the murder weapon was stolen from a military or government stockpile. Except that by treaty, there weren't supposed to be any such stockpiles.

There were, however, three previous deaths that may have involved this nerve agent. The reports were not conclusive. In two cases the bodies had subsequently been badly burned in fires that may have been set to cover up the murders. In the third case, the body had been found in the late stages of decay. But in all three there were traces of one or the other of the two parts of the binary toxin.

I sent Sam a quick note, asking what these three deaths might have in common. He would have data inaccessible to me, and I would not be drawing attention to myself with my own search.

In the search for local facilities and people who could be capable of doing germ line genetic modifications and mitochondrial replacement, there was a long list. I did not trust the list much, since my name appeared on it, a couple pages down. The two major west coast longevity centers were high on the list. They were both racing to move mitochondrial DNA into the nucleus of the cell, so that nuclear DNA repair mechanisms could protect those genes from the kind of damage associated with a host of age-related diseases. They would probably need a mechanism for removing all traces of a gene from all the mitochondria, so that they could assess the function of the nuclear DNA replacement. But neither of them had published yet, meaning either that a patent would give away too much information to the other company, or that they had made no progress. Since I was interested in technologies available 24 years ago, this appeared to be a dead end either way.

The computer had drawn a web of connections between the people and companies on the list, and Jonathan Worthington. Not surprisingly, there were several knots of connections. People shared workplaces, co-authored papers (generally with several hundred co-authors, indicating a company-wide research project), or went to school with one another.

On a hunch, I ran a quick search for public records of grants and other funding sources for each of the people on the list, including Worthington. I overlaid that graph on the connection graph, and looked for holes, places where there were knots of connections, but no funding on record for the period between 26 and 24 years ago. One bright knot showed up unpainted by visible funds. Seventeen people connected with one company, apparently funding the project solely with private company funds. Jonathan Worthington was not on the list of the seventeen, but he was closely related with eight of them. The company, California Biomed Laboratories, had declared bankruptcy four months after Catrina Worthington was born.

I love coincidences. Life was suddenly getting very interesting. I sent the list and some notes to Sam.

Downstairs, the smell of chicken broth was filling the kitchen. The pressure cooker was rattling and hissing as it dissolved the chicken bones. Cat was chopping carrots and celery. I took the broth off the heat and filtered out what remained of the chicken bones in a large strainer, and put the clear broth back on the stove, adding the bag of herbs, the sautéed meat, and the vegetables.

While the soup cooked, I made some cornbread, and Cat made a salad. It was unlikely that Becca would be able to hold down the salad, but the chicken soup and maybe a small bit of cornbread should stay put. We carried the dinner on trays up to Becca's room.

Becca had a wildlife show playing on the screen in front of the bed, and we watched flocks of birds and prides of lions as we ate. I filled them in on what I had found out, but none of the people or the company name meant anything to them. It had all happened before they were born.

Cat stayed to watch the end while I collected dishes and took them downstairs. I had cleaned up, and was in bed about to drift off to sleep when I heard Cat come into my room quietly. She crawled into bed next to me. I rolled over to let her snuggle in tight, but she made it clear without a word that she had not come in to sleep. A little over an hour later, sweaty and relieved, we both lay on the sheets with the covers at the foot of the bed. My bed does not have a wall to bang against, but I was sure we'd made enough noise to keep Becca up-to-date on new sleeping arrangements. I slept very well that night, a warm slender body next to mine.

§

Chapter Fourteen

The next morning, I got a call from Sam.

"Got a hit on your list," he said. "A guy named Jason Mallory. A gang hit, throat sliced from ear to ear, apparently after torture. Burns and bruises, crude stuff. Happened five weeks ago, still being investigated. Best guess at this point is he was on the bad side of a right-wing neo-Nazi organized crime group from down south. But that's not the kicker. Guess who he was seeing a lot of in the last seven months before his death? Margaret Jackson."

"So, we have a third murder," I said. "Any idea how they relate?"

"Not a clue. Nothing connects this group to anyone on your list, and these aren't high tech weenies, these are thugs. Really bad news. Into drugs mostly, some recreational stuff but mostly athletic performance enhancers, selling to high school wrestling teams and body builders, that kind of shit. They take a lot of their own dope, these guys look like someone pumped them up and skinned them alive, all ripped muscle and tendon. Covered in prison tats. The kind of thing you don't want to run into in a dark alley. Give you nightmares."

"What's the name of the organization?" I asked.

"They call themselves October Nine, after the privacy riots. Used to be all about protecting the cash economy, now it's just a hate group, trying to return the U.S. to a majority white population. Nut cases held together by the profits from the illegal supplement trade."

I was quickly entering all of this information into a new search program. Sam had access to data that I didn't have, but he was constrained by strict privacy laws from doing searches that are available to me, as a private citizen. Not that many private citizens had my resources, access, or particular skills. Sam knew I could help, but he could not ask for my help. He could just feed me information, and trust my curiosity and competitive nature.

"Roland Drake had no visible tattoos," I said. "Did your people check for signs of removal? It would be interesting to see if he had any shared prison experiences with October Nine."

"I'll get on that. We can check prison records too, see who was with him, cross correlate with October Nine members. You thinking he was a face man for them?" Sam asked.

"It's worth checking out. See if any of their enhancers show up in his blood work, too. My gut says that Roland Drake was working for whoever killed Jason Mallory. And my research is leading me to believe that he was killed by someone *not* working for them. Worse, that same research is coming up blank on connections between the nerve agent and the genetics group. We might be dealing with three different interest groups, all connected by Margaret Jackson."

"Any of that research something I could use in a warrant?" Sam asked, knowing the answer before I spoke.

"Not a bit. Legal, but not admissible," I said, confirming his pessimism.

When Sam disconnected, I looked over the data that had come up on the screen from my most recent search. Jason Mallory was a low-level technician working for a Massachusetts genetics firm called GenePharm. The search program had been analyzing links in social network companies, and had come up with two subnetworks of associations. One was related to coworkers in biotechnology firms, but the other was more tenuous, resembling links between people based on sexual orientation or some other connection that is normally not advertised. Since the genders of the people in the network were evenly distributed, they were most likely linked by some common secret other than sexual orientation. I instructed the computer to look for common psychological disorders, histories of child abuse, common criminal records, alcoholism, drug use, and other categories of possible shared experiences that people would not ordinarily advertise. The answer came up immediately. There was a 93 percent chance that these people went to the same Alcoholics Anonymous meetings at a church on Center Street.

Margaret Jackson and James Mallory shared an addiction. Had she met him at the meeting, or at the liquor store where she worked? He did not live close to the liquor store. It could be that he went to stores away from his local neighborhood to avoid his neighbors when making purchases, but it seemed more likely that they met at the church. I entered this bit of surmise into the search program.

I looked up the local offices of GenePharm. Surprisingly, there were none. The nearest office was a small sales office in Texas. All research and development took place in Massachusetts. What was a genetics technician doing this far from the lab? This is not work that is generally done remotely.

I ran a search on GenePharm employees within 50 miles of Jason Mallory's house. A familiar list of people showed up. I compared this list with the network of seventeen people with no public grants. There was a high level of overlap. The new names were probably non-technical employees.

I sent the new information to Sam, and sent the list of local GenePharm employees to Jacob, asking him to have someone follow them to work, to find out where they spent their days.

Both Becca and I had shrink appointments that day. I had not discussed what my meetings were about, and neither of the women had asked. I told Cat she could take the two-seater up the coast, and drive manually if she liked on the winding roads, while getting

Becca to her appointment on time. I took the modest sedan I drove when I wanted to attract little or no attention.

Doctor Hoffman's receptionist again tried to find something to do that did not involve speaking to me. She could not avoid secretly glancing at me from time to time, and I pretended not to notice. I read the diplomas on the wall again, something I never have to do, but something that would go without notice. The doctor's full name was Howard Herbert Hoffman. I wondered what kind of mother would do that to a child, and whether it had any influence on his choice of profession.

The doctor came out to meet me, smiled wordlessly at the receptionist, and we entered his office. He sat down next to the monitor, and I relaxed in the big padded chair. He studied the monitor as if deciding which of many questions to ask. I interpreted this as dramatic pause, since he would clearly have decided long ago.

"I'd like to discuss your relationship with your brother's wife, Catherine," he said. Clearly this time he had been doing his homework, watching videos of prior sessions in other offices, and reading transcripts and notes.

"His first wife," I said.

"He's had more than one?" Hoffman asked, worried that this bit of information had escaped his notice.

"Not yet," I said.

"You don't approve of this marriage," he said, comforted that his preparation had been adequate after all.

"He married her for her looks," I said. "He'll marry the second one for her looks as well. By the third wife, he'll finally marry for something meaningful, like companionship and compatible philosophies, and then he'll be happy. But the third wife will still be a looker."

"You hold her good looks against her?"

"Not at all. I enjoy good looking women. In general. This particular one annoys me."

"That seems to be a common thread in your relationships," he said.

"This relationship is my brother's, not mine," I pointed out.

"One which you tried to sabotage?"

"No. There's no point in that. He's going to follow the pattern, and I'll just have to wait for number three," I said.

"But there has been considerable friction, nonetheless," he pointed out.

"Of course. If she hadn't been drop-dead gorgeous, Sam would never have had a thing to do with her. She barely made it through college, she went after Sam so she could marry up, something that was incredibly important to her, so she could look down on everyone she had grown up with back in Texas. He is her only accomplishment, and she's ridiculously proud of that."

"She seems to have a wide variety of charitable and philanthropic activities. You don't think of those as accomplishments?"

"She does those so she can throw parties and invite wealthy people. So that her name will be in the papers back home. She could give a damn about Cambodian orphans."

"You don't approve of the woman, or the marriage, but you never did anything to prevent the wedding from taking place?"

"I did some things to protect my brother, and myself, from gold-diggers. But nothing specifically to prevent her from marrying him."

"Let's talk about some of those protective measures," he said.

"She liked the house. For all the wrong reasons. Sam and I were still living in the house our parents built. It has substantial senti-mental value to both of us, but it also has some very important fea-tures, such as privacy, security, location, and specialized work spaces. The one thing Sam and I always hated about the house was the front entrance. A huge waste of space, designed as conspicuous consumption, aimed at intimidating people. Mom hated it too. Dad needed it that way for business reasons, or so he thought, and the architect absolutely loved it. Sam and I always use one of the back entrances, usually the garage. But Catherine loved it. She hardly noticed the rest of the place, which is functionally designed to be a perfect living and working space. For her, show was all that was important."

"And you didn't like that," he said. I ignored the comment. It was useless filler, shrink talk for 'Tell me more about your mother'.

"Sam and I had inherited the house and the company and a bunch of other things, all equally. We both knew that one of us would have to move out of the house. The main value was in the company, of course, and the house, while of significant value, was minor in comparison. I made Sam a deal. In front of Catherine. I would trade him my share of the company for his share of the house."

"And he obviously took the deal."

"He was really pissed. He hates it when I manipulate him. He hates it when I point out he is making a bad choice. Catherine was com-pletely transparent, we could both read the calculations going on in her face. She would lose the house, but she would gain billions of dollars, and her husband would be much richer than the annoying brother-in-law. This one deal would put her into the Forbes 400 richest people in the world, something that, of the three of us, only she cared about in the least."

"He was upset, even though he was getting the best side of a hugely lopsided arrangement?"

"It meant he would have a controlling interest in Xenocor. That meant all the obligations and responsibilities of running a huge corporation, when all he wanted to do was find the people who killed Dad. And Catherine was going to insist that he take the deal, and be the guy running Xenocor."

"Was that all he was upset about?"

"Well, no. But he didn't realize the thing about the pre-nup until much later."

"There was a pre-nuptial agreement?" he asked.

"It's a provision of Dad's will. Holds for both of us. I helped Jacob write it up, ostensibly to make sure it corresponded to the wording in the will. In actuality, Jake and I made it pretty strict, but it still looked like she would get a big chunk if the marriage didn't work out. They had both signed it, and I had to sign off as well, as part of the provisions in the will. And I had. But neither of them counted on the timing, which was crucial. The wedding was in February. We closed the deal on the house and Xenocor in January, which set the terms of the pre-nup. But Sam would have to sell a bunch of Xenocor stock to pay the taxes on the deal, since the house wasn't worth one percent of the Xenocor stock I was giving up. That sale didn't have to take place until April 15th of the following year. Since the pre-nup protected everything that Sam owned prior to the signing, and he would be a billion and a half poorer after selling the stock to pay taxes, she will essentially get nothing at all if the marriage breaks up."

"And you knew all of this at the time?"

"Of course."

"And you don't consider that sabotaging their relationship?" Hoffman asked.

"Just the opposite. Now she has every reason to stay married to Sam. She'll have nothing if she blows that. She'll have to line up some other sucker with money if she wants out, while she still has her looks."

"You still haven't mentioned the dog and the lipstick," Hoffman said.

"That wasn't me. I'm completely innocent on that one."

"But it apparently caused more of the friction than either of the other two protective measures you undertook."

I smiled. He had heard what I said to three other shrinks about this. He had read their notes. But he wanted me to explain it again. He probably knew by now that I would explain it differently, as I had each previous time, even though the facts were always the same. I hate repeating myself, and I never forget what I've said before.

Catherine was building her dream house as far away from Dad's house as Sam would let her. It was across the valley, and on a clear day I could see the construction going on with a telescope if I had wanted to. Both houses were in the hills overlooking the valley, but hers was to be slightly higher. The design was a mess, full of conflicting styles and periods, as if she had gone through an architecture book and picked out all the things she liked without regard as to how they went together. It was also huge, and there were several newspaper articles about suspected improprieties in the zoning and permitting, all but alleging bribery. There probably would have been bribery if not for Sam's firm hand.

When the house was finally completed, none of the three architects wanted to take any credit for it, each blaming the other or the owners for the final result. But it was everything Catherine wanted in a house, big, showy, and everything obviously very expensive. There was a huge party at the opening, and anyone with money, power, or fame was on the guest list. Even I received an invitation, although I suspect Catherine hoped I would not attend. Which may have been why I decided to go.

I put a great deal of planning into the selection of a date for the party. I had six weeks of notice, and I put it to good use, not only selecting the person, but arranging to meet her and get to know her before asking her to join me at the party.

Of course, it had to be a famous super model. Someone Catherine would not want to be compared to in the press. I invested in a clothing design company and some fashion magazines, and arranged to be present at a photo shoot in Cancun. Everyone wanted to meet the new boss, and even I can be charming when my competitive nature demands it.

What I hadn't counted on was that she would be bright and interesting. She had a reputation for being the spoiled incorrigible prima donna, and I was quite surprised to find that the act hid a mind that was responsible for her career success and business acumen. During our first dinner together, she pretended to drink and to get drunk, but I could not help noticing that she ordered new drinks well before the old was barely touched, and that the drinks always were mostly ice, and that she spilled a lot. Very cleverly done. It would have fooled almost anyone else.

The drunken facade let her do things and ask questions that would have raised eyebrows in other situations. But the things she asked or did always kept her in control of the situation, and gave her insights she would not have gotten otherwise. It also allowed her to more easily use sex to get what she wanted, and I was all in favor of that. Her career advanced measurably in only two weeks of traveling with me. Magazines (including those I now owned) delighted in running pictures of us at various exotic locations.

I had warned her that our hostess might snub her brother-in-law and his gorgeous guest, and she seemed to take some delight in the idea of a counter attack. My work done, we attended the affair in a new limousine, one I still own to this day, and even use occasionally.

We actually had fun at the party. Cherrie at my side, we gathered a knot of gossip press and well-dressed women, and she kept them aghast with stories about people in the fashion industry behaving badly, while making a show of drinking and slowly having trouble walking, and in general behaving like the people in her stories. She was making quite an impression.

When we finally did run into our hosts, Catherine had been getting reports about Cherrie for over an hour. Catherine was standing on the first step of one of the huge staircases leading from the central ballroom, which is the only thing that made her taller than Cherrie. She used this advantage to stiffly look down her nose at the apparently drunken celebrity, and put on a weak smile that was intended to show politeness barely concealing contempt. I was a few feet away getting Cherrie another drink when Catherine bent over and whispered something in her ear. The noise in the room prevented any real whispering, of course, and the five or six people nearby could plainly hear what was said. They looked surprised and startled by the exchange.

Cherrie looked startled for a moment, although I knew she had been wanting something just like this to happen. Then she tilted her head back and laughed as if Catherine had told her a really

funny joke. She turned to her audience and apologized for Catherine. "She's not really a bitch. You can always tell. Dogs wear better lipstick." The crowd appreciated this and laughed with her, and
she drifted away with them.

None of this exchange would have made it into a gossip sheet, let
alone the evening news. But Catherine had made a big deal of
dressing up her large poodle in the same ribbons and curly hair
style as Catherine herself. And when at the end of the evening, the
dog was seen wearing a large smile painted on using Cherrie's shade
of lipstick, the photographers and video people had a field day. The
papers and the evening news showed pictures of Catherine and the
dog side by side, and the video of Catherine insulting Cherrie in
front of reporters, and Cherrie's response were all that the news
covered.

Hoffman considered all of this. "And you hold that you were completely innocent in this affair?"

"Doc, I was designed to be competitive. It's in my blood, in my
genes. And I always win."

"And Cherrie Winston is now running three magazines owned by
you."

"And doing a great job. Did I mention how much money she is
making for me?"

He paused, letting this sink in, and entered some notes. Then he
did one of his gratuitous dramatic pauses, which I took as a signal
he was changing subjects.

"You mentioned the Forbes 400, saying that you and your brother
had no interest in that. And yet you say you are highly competitive.
How do you reconcile those two statements."

"We had no interest because neither of us were on the list," I said.

"But that is no longer the case."

"True," I admitted.

"It is unlike you to respond in monosyllables. When did you first appear on that list?" he asked.

"April 15th, after the wedding."

"Another terse reply. When was your brother on the list?"

"From the day he got Xenocor for the house, until April 15th, after the wedding," I said.

"And this curious timing was due to what, exactly?"

I smiled. "Someone had gotten on the list."

"And you had to win. But you knew your brother would be off the list after he had paid his taxes."

"Actually, he was off the list the moment the deal was made, since he paid estimated taxes on the earnings at the time they were reported. So technically, he was only on the list for a day," I explained.

"But you went to the trouble of tripling your personal wealth in four months," he said. "That must have taken enormous effort, even for you."

"I didn't have a lot of time for anything else, if that's what you mean," I said.

"But you didn't stop there. You had won, but you did it again, tripling your wealth during the next four months."

"Once might have been a fluke. I had to prove to myself I could do it anytime I liked."

"To yourself?" Now Hoffman was giving short replies.

"At that point, yes," I said. "When something is hard to do, I usually do it twice, to eliminate chance. I do that for my own pride. Did I tell you pride was one of my sins?"

"And Catherine's feelings about being on the list had nothing to do with it?"

"Not the second time. There are two important places to be for her. *On* the list, or at the *top*."

"But you are not at the top, are you?" he said rhetorically.

"She's unlikely to ever be at the top, so there's no point, as far as competing with her is concerned."

"But now you are on the list. Aren't you competing with the entire world?"

"I only compete for things that are important to me. For that it usually has to be personal."

"But in fact, you've been at number 22 on that list ever since you proved that getting on the list was not a fluke. This is curious to people who collect statistics. There is a lot of flux in that area of the list, and yet your place has been at number 22 for years. You are still trying to prove something with that, are you not?"

I smiled again. "Being first would mean that money is important. It isn't, it is just a way to keep score in a game that only mildly amuses me. Being second would mean losing that game. Being forever third would not be much better. So, pick a time to quit, and that's your number. Staying at that number proves to yourself, and anyone paying attention, that you could be at any number you wish. That is how you win a game like that."

"And you've won the wealth game, in your mind."

"No. Wealth is real. Wealth is something you can do things with, something you can use to change the world. I won the pissing contest. Wealth is not a game."

§

Chapter Fifteen

Cat and Becca were not back yet when I returned home. There was a message from Jacob, however. His people had found what they believed was Margaret Jackson's rooftop home away from home. They were staking it out waiting for her to return.

The right thing to do at this point was to inform Sam and let him do his own stakeout. However, this was something I wanted to talk to her daughters about before taking any action myself. Sam might not be able to protect her perfectly, but she did not seem to be in the safest situation at the moment either.

It was quiet without the company I had enjoyed over the past ten days. I smiled, knowing that I had indeed enjoyed it, and thinking what Sam would say if he knew. It was a sure bet that no one at the precinct had picked a number as large as ten in the pool. But the quiet was disquieting, and I went downstairs to the music room and sat down at the piano.

I had been working on a composition before my life became a little more complicated, and I played it again, but this time made some changes, adding mystery and a little melancholy, reflecting the moods of the last week and a half. The result was much more satisfactory than the first version, which was precise and mathematical, playing with 5/4 timing and subtle harmonies. These were still there, but had new color, and where before I had stopped, stumped as to where to take the piece, now there was new life, and the composition became clear. I recorded the finished piano part, and picked up the guitar and explored the main theme again, against the recording.

"That's pretty good," said Cat, leaning against the doorway. Becca was behind her.

"How did it go with Clay?" I asked, beckoning them into the room.

"He's happy," Becca said, slumping on the floor against the wall. "I looked up the Manheim Protocol, you asshole." She fingered the steel vial around her neck.

"Did it work for you?" I asked.

"They said it was unethical, and nobody used it anymore."

"Clay Garret has his own ethics. He is concerned with results. Did it work for you?"

"You mean did I take the pill? No, I didn't, asshole. I sweated through the whole damned thing, holding on to my last hope like an idiot. The fucking hardest thing I ever did, and you just watched, when you *knew*. Asshole."

"So then he was right," I said.

"He's an asshole too. I could have slept through the whole damn thing!"

Cat interrupted. "What is the Manheim Protocol?" she asked.

"It's a fucking lie!" Becca said.

"Yes," I said. "That's why some consider it unethical. The pill she has around her neck is a fast-acting sleeping pill. It would have kept her asleep for about 48 hours, long enough for the effects of withdrawal to be mostly over with. She was told that it was only to be used as a last resort, and that it would only work once, and that if she ever needed it again, it would not be available. In a sense, that is true, since a lie only works once."

Cat looked puzzled. "Why bother? Why not just give her the pill?"

I looked over at Becca. "She knows. Don't you, Becca."

Becca gave me an angry look, but then nodded.

"She wanted to be free of her addiction. She wanted it so badly that she went through hell to do it. She knew that the pill would make the hell go away, but she was looking to the future. She will always be able to look back on that experience, and know that getting rid of the addiction was once worth so much to her that she went through all of that. And that knowledge will help her avoid slipping back into old habits."

"I'm keeping the pill, you know," Becca said to me.

I nodded, and picked up the guitar. The piano recording began again as I laid out an arpeggio, picking up at just the right place. Cat slid onto the piano bench and looked for sheet music, and, not finding any, she closed her eyes and listened to the piece. Her fingers went to the keyboard, and she filled in some harmony gently, tentatively exploring the sounds. I picked up those notes on the guitar and expanded it into a theme. Encouraged, she became less shy at the keys, and innovated, staying within the patterns of rhythm and chords, but adding a less somber, more playful mood.

The piece was short, and the ending was foreseeable, and she stopped her part and let the original piano part play out. I held the guitar in my lap, and regarded her.

"It needs something," she said when the recording ended.

"The mystery part isn't solved," I said.

"It needs to get out of the minor key. Have a happy ending."

"That would be nice, wouldn't it?" I replied.

Becca stood up. "You two are full of it," she said, grinning, and sat down beside her sister and started playing "Heart and Soul". Cat laughed, and played along with her sister, the events of the last few days temporarily forgotten.

I waited for them to finish. "Jacob thinks he's found where your mother has been staying," I said.

Becca looked up cautiously. "Where?"

"On the roof of the office supply store on Fifth. He's got it staked out. He'll call when they see her."

"You mean nobody has actually seen her," Cat said. "We don't know if she's all right."

"Not yet," I said.

"What's the plan?" Becca asked, eyeing me closely.

"That's up to you. She's probably in some amount of danger. She's wanted by the police, but she hasn't done anything illegal, apart from camping out on the roof, and perhaps stealing something that Roland Drake wanted. Sam can process her as a Jane Doe, perhaps keep her safe. She's not very safe where she is."

"What if we just got her on a plane and flew back to Maryland?" Becca asked.

"That's an option. Someone may be watching airports. We don't know what resources they have available to them, or how important she is to them. But these are people with access to illegal military nerve agents, and sophisticated laboratories. They are not without funds, and they have killed three people so far."

"Three?" Cat asked. "I thought it was two."

"A man named Jason Mallory was beat up and murdered about five weeks ago. Apparently tortured and burned. He was a friend of your mother's. They may have been dating. They may have met at an AA meeting. And he's mixed up in whatever is going on. He's a technician at a lab somewhere here in the city."

"When did you learn all this?" Becca asked.

"This morning, before you left for Garret's. I thought it best to wait."

"You're such a patronizing shithead. I'm not that fragile," Becca said, eyes narrowing.

"You're right. I apologize. I learned about your mother only minutes before you came back."

"Could we keep her here?" Cat asked.

"We could. But we really should tell Sam. He has three murders he's investigating, and we really should not get in his way. For one thing it would not be legal, but more importantly, it would not be right, and it would not be in your mother's best interest. Helping Sam get the bad guys is the best way to keep her safe."

"Can we let Mom decide?" Becca asked.

"We should let Sam know what we know as soon as possible. He can have people watch the building, make sure she's safe."

"Bec," Cat began. Becca interrupted. "Ok, ok, we call Sam. This shit is getting way over our heads."

We walked into the media room to place the call. Cat and Becca sat on either side of me on the couch in front of the big screen. I was surprised when Sam answered the call, in person. He must have been working late. Sam seemed equally surprised to see the women with me.

"Hi, Sam," I began. "We think we might know where Margaret Jackson has been, at least recently. I have some people discreetly watching the roof of the OfficeMart on Fifth. I thought you might want to discreetly join them."

He was silent for a moment, still looking at the women on either side of me. "How the hell would she get onto the roof of the OfficeMart?" he asked, eventually.

"Apparently it's a trick she's used before when she wanted to avoid attention. She'd likely bolt if she saw a cruiser in the area."

"I know what discreet means, J.T.," Sam said, with a tired voice.

"You're working late," I said.

"Yeah. The Chinese consulate is all upset. They heard that those October Nine nuts had been working north. They're putting a lot of political pressure on. They believe all that shit about a tailored race-targeting virus." Sam gave a small sigh and looked down at the paperwork on his desk.

"Why would they be worried about a virus in this day and age? Everybody takes a broad-spectrum antiviral at the first sign of sniffles," I said.

"Who knows. Could be an engineered virus could get around that. Speaking of which, my lab guys say they're finding signed viral traces just about everywhere Jonathan Worthington goes. You wouldn't know anything about that, would you? Maybe someone slipped into his hotel room and replaced his bottle of DayVir with a placebo?" Sam managed to look even more tired as he spoke.

"I'm sure you'll find a licensed epidemiological research firm when you check out the signatures. Probably one owned by Xenocor, they're the best at that. I'd think you'd appreciate someone making your job a little easier."

"Don't make this a competition, J.T., these goons are dangerous. Stupid dangerous, so you can't count on them being predictable or doing sane things. Don't go figuring you've got them pegged, they don't always behave logically." Sam looked at the two women beside me as if he were trying to convince them instead of me.

"Have you made any headway on the other two actors in this party?" I asked.

"You still think there's more to it than the O9 fuckups?" Sam said, suddenly taking me more seriously.

"October Nine would have to outsource anything technical. So what Margaret Jackson was hiding in the freezer was not likely taken from October Nine, but from some intermediary. Roland Drake took it, so he's either with the intermediary, or with October Nine. My bet is the latter, since we have no reason to think the intermediary would murder, whereas October Nine has no qualms about noisily letting people know what happens if they aren't cooperative. Then there is the party who took out Roland Drake. That is most likely a third party. They have access to exotic weapons, and don't mind killing, so they aren't in either of the first two groups."

"Not very convincing, J.T. There's nothing there I can work with. It's all conjecture. But you let me know when you get something concrete."

"I'm working on that," I said.

"Leave it to the professionals, J.T." Sam warned.

"Absolutely," I said. "The best that money can buy."

"Yes," Sam said. "I heard that Barnaby Wilson was in town, spending a lot of money."

"I'm afraid Mr. Wilson and I are not on a first name basis," I said.

"If my name was Barnaby, I'd never use it either. Good to know he's on our side in this."

"So far," I said. "In the end, that may come down to what interest the DA has in Margaret Jackson or Jonathan Worthington."

"I'll take that as a warning, J.T. And what's it been now, ten days?" he said, surreptitiously glancing at Becca and Cat.

I ignored the glance. "Since the first murder? No, I think the first one was Jason Mallory. That would be 47 days, 10 hours, plus or minus the coroner's margin of error."

"Pretty amazing," he said, ignoring my feint. "A new record every day." He waved goodbye, and the screen went back to pretending to be a Mondrian.

I called Jacob. He answered voice only, with sounds of a restaurant in the background.

"Sam's folks will be joining the watch at the OfficeMart. And apparently the Chinese consulate is putting pressure on them to do something about the local October Nine infestation. You might want to watch the consulate and anyone having business with the consulate, and see if any of them are sniffing around where your folks are. Someone with access to binary nerve toxins took out Roland Drake, and it looks to me like the Chinese government may be taking vermin eradication into its own hands. I'm going to forward your office some data on the catalyst and the substrate so you can arm your people with sniffers, in case they try the nerve agent again."

"I'll let the troops know," Jacob said.

"Have a nice dinner," I said, and disconnected.

Later that night, Cat propped her elbow on the pillow and looked down at me. "So, should I feel special?" she asked.

"I should think so," I said, tucking a strand of hair behind her ear.

"A new record every day," she said.

"Pay no attention to Sam," I said.

"I don't know," she said, rolling over on top of me. "I kind of like feeling special."

"Sometimes," I said, "I do too."

§

Chapter Sixteen

Margaret Jackson did not return to the roof of the OfficeMart that night. Neither Sam nor Jacob were surprised. But by the time breakfast was all cleaned up, Becca was getting upset.

"I can't just sit around waiting for something to happen. I want to go out and *do* something." She was still recovering, and it was difficult to tell whether her agitation was due to the withdrawal, the various medications Garret had her on, cabin fever, or genuine concern for her estranged mother's welfare. Nonetheless, the three of us started to plan our day around doing some private sleuthing.

Sam had tried to get useful information from the remaining employees at the liquor store, but had had no luck. Likewise, Jacob's people had struck out. But both of them had come at them in official mode, and I thought a softer approach was worth a try.

I was hesitant about our choice of vehicle. The non-descript sedan was an obvious choice, and would allow us to move around without arousing suspicion. But the limousine had certain security features I was hoping never to need. Cat made the decision. "Fuck the limo. We'll stay sharper if we don't think we're safe." Apparently, she shared her sister's risk-taking profile, genetic or not.

She also took what we still anachronistically call the driver's seat, although the trip would be fully automatic, since the trip would be mostly city driving. Becca sat up front, leaving me with the back seat. We set off towards Lawrence Liquors. Once we were on the road, Cat swiveled her seat around to face me in the back.

"Jacob isn't really a lawyer, *is* he?" she asked.

"Of course he is," I said.

"I mean, he's a lawyer like you're a lawyer. Got the degree and all, but that's not his job."

"I value his legal acumen, but he has teams of people that do the actual gruntwork. He's very creative, and he manages people extremely well. And he likes to get his hands dirty. He enjoys it when surprises happen, and he's very hands-on."

"That's what Susan said," Becca snickered. She swiveled her seat around also.

"You don't like puppets on strings, *do* you?" Cat said.

"I prefer autonomous agents. Let them know what the goal is, make sure they have what they need, and then stay out of their way."

"Fire and forget, like a cruise missile," Cat said.

"More like an automobile. Tell it where you want to be, and sit back and think about something else," I said.

"I like to drive," Cat said. Becca and I laughed together.

We parked a couple doors down from the liquor store. I wanted to go in first, get a look around, before the women came in.

The police tape was gone, the wall behind the register was patched and painted, and for the most part you would never know anything had happened. But I immediately noticed the extra security measures. There were four extra cameras, of high quality, and a jump screen had been installed in front of the register, so the clerk could have a bullet-proof wall between her and the customer in an instant if the need should arise. The screen next to the clerk showed images of each customer as the cameras silently tracked their movements.

I walked around the store, leaving no area unscanned, and selected a bottle of Southern Comfort and placed it on the counter. Then, as if forgetting something, I went to the back of the store where the freezers were, and took out a box of Drumsticks.

By the time I returned, Cat and Becca had seen the signal and were talking to the clerk at the register. I put the ice cream down by the bottle.

Cat looked up at me. "My mom loves that stuff," she said, pointing to the bottle of Southern Comfort. She looked back at the clerk. "Do you know my mom? Margaret Jackson?"

The clerk ignored me, fascinated by Cat. "You're the two kids in the picture! The one she keeps taped to the door on her locker! Shit, that picture must be really old." His eyes moved from Cat's face to Becca's cleavage and back.

"We're trying to find her. The shitheads at the police are useless," she leaned closer to the clerk. "Do you know anyone who might help her if she was in trouble? Any friends?"

The clerk glanced at me, and I suddenly remembered I needed a magazine. I turned and walked towards the newsstand, listening carefully.

"She was really tight with that Jason fuck, 'til he got sliced up in that mugging. He was bad for her though, a real alky. She had hers under control, unless he was around. She'd come in to work with a little buzz on, and maybe get a little lit on her break, but that fuck was hard core. You could drive a semi across the country on his breath."

"Anyone else? I hear Jason isn't drinking anymore."

The clerk laughed out loud, and slapped the counter hard. Regaining his composure, he said "There was some other wanky guy that hung around Jason sometimes. Jerry something. He worked with Jason, loaned him money for a bottle every once in a while. She used to hit on him when she was lit. By then Jason was usually useless. I don't mean to talk shit about your mom, you know, she was really cool, she just liked to party, you know?"

Cat smiled. "That's Mom. Good for her! Do you know where we might find this Jerry guy?"

The clerk shook his head. "Nah, I haven't seen that wank since that Jason guy stopped coming in."

Cat put her arm on the counter and leaned in towards the clerk. "Thanks a lot, anyway. You've been a big help. Is it OK if I call you sometime, in case I think of something else I need to ask?"

He quickly grabbed a piece of receipt tape and wrote down his phone number. Cat tucked it into her bra and waved a cute little goodbye, and took Becca by the hand and left the store. I picked up a men's magazine, and went to the counter to make my purchase. The clerk looked at the magazine, and then up at me. "Hey, did you check out the centerfold? That is one endowed dude, I tell you."

I paid for the items and walked back to the car. Inside, I handed the bag to Becca and told the car to head for a nicer neighborhood as I placed a call to Jacob.

"Do we have a photo and address for Jerry Lawson?" I asked when his face showed up on the screen. Lawson was one of the privately funded seventeen people connected to California Biomed Laboratories and Jonathan Worthington.

"I can do better than that," he said. "I think I know where he works. But he didn't come in this morning with the rest. Six of the people on your list entered a small building in the biotech park at Bayside. No logo, no lobby, good security, all automated. No one to talk to. No deliveries yet today. We're canvassing the local lunch places, talking to workers in nearby buildings, but it will take a while if we stay discreet. "

"That's a long way from Lawrence Liquors. What would bring Lawson and Mallory out this way?"

"Mallory lived out there," Jacob said. "And his AA group met in the church a few blocks from the store. Looks like Ms. Jackson chose the area to be close to him. From the timeline we're building up, it looks like she moved into the neighborhood before they hooked up, so she may have been targeting him. Too many coincidences otherwise."

Jerry Lawson's address came up on the screen, and I redirected the car.

"We're heading over to Lawson's," I said to Jacob. "We'll ring the bell and say the liquor store clerk sent us, see what's up," I said.

"Keep an eye out for Jonathan Worthington. The sniffers say he's been in that area. We're a little undermanned at the moment, and we put him on sniffer only since we've got him tagged. But that means we don't have minute to minute location data for him." Jacob seemed a little contrite, as if admitting he was short handed was embarrassing to him. The screen went blank as he disconnected.

Cat looked over at me. "I really don't feel like meeting up with Dad right now."

"He could answer a lot of questions," I said.

"If he wanted to answer those questions, he's had 24 years to do it. He might be out here trying to make sure those questions never get answered."

That thought had occurred to me earlier.

Becca passed out ice cream. "This stuff's going to melt if we don't eat it."

"The limo has a freezer," I said.

"Good thing we didn't take the limo then," Cat said, reaching for the ice cream.

Becca had opened the magazine. She held it up so the centerfold fell out. Then she started laughing out loud. "Cat, look!" she said, nearly losing her bite of ice cream in her laughter. "It's Marvin the Geek!"

Cat gasped as she saw the picture, and doubled over laughing. "You're right! That is so rag!"

I looked at the picture. There was an attractive, if over-engineered young woman, and an extremely well-endowed young man.

"Who is Marvin the Geek?" I asked, and the two women doubled over again in explosive laughter. It took Cat several seconds to recover her breath. She had tears in her eyes as she struggled to get the words out.

"We thought," she said, and took a quick breath, "that he would be harmless."

"He was my second Trip," said Becca, "so we wanted someone easy, someone Cat could control if he got too..."

"...excited," Cat finished. They doubled over again, in uncontrollable giggles.

"He was nice," Becca said. "And completely disposable. Total dweeb. So, we take him back to the dorm and I drop some T, and I'm thinking he's my superman, my hero, some gorgeous Prince Charming, and I'm not surprised that I can't get my mouth around it. When you're on T, you focus on anything unusual, and that

becomes the most wonderful thing in the world. So here he is..."
and she lost her ability to speak again, drawing in big gasps of air.

"...with his feet straight up in the air," said Cat. "Becca called me in
to see this wonderful thing, so I burst into the room, and he's lying
on the bed, no pants on, feet straight up, and Becca's still trying to
get it into her mouth..."

"...and he sees her and gets embarrassed, and puts his feet down..."
Becca continued.

"...and he passes out cold. The thing is so fat he can't get enough
blood to his brain unless his feet are up in the air. And I'm looking
at this, wondering whether I should call a doctor or just roll on the
floor laughing, and Becca is sitting on top of him asking me to help
her get it in. She's gonna make him happy even if he's sleeping
through the whole thing." Cat said, wiping her eyes.

"Cat walks out and leaves me there with him, and I'm trying to get
his legs up and his thing in, wishing I had like a gallon of lube or
something, and he wakes up and tries to help. But he's never done
it before, even by himself because he keeps passing out. He finally
gets a rhythm going and scores even though it isn't in, not in the
slightest, and he passes out again. But I'm so tripped, it's like my
job to keep doing him all night, and as soon as he comes to, it swells
up again, and he can't think straight, and I get him to pop off again
finally, and he conks out. I think I have the trick now, and I pop
him off like every 20 minutes all night long, and he can hardly get
his breath all night. I start coming down, and my muscles ache
from riding him all night, and I slide off. He comes to, and sees me
lying there, and he bolts out of bed and out the door, and he never
came back for his pants." Becca dissolved into giggles again, and
Cat let her head fall back on the headrest and drew in big gasps of
air.

"I missed all my classes that day," Becca said, "I slept until two in the afternoon, and even then, I could barely walk, from leg cramps and arm cramps from holding his damn legs up in the air all night. Cat had to help me get to the toilet. We never saw Marvin again, not around campus, not around town, nothing. He just disappeared."

"Just as well, since Becca had a plan to put him into a coma by slipping him some limp dick pills," Cat said.

Becca paused, lost in thought.

"My first was my boyfriend. He scored a bunch of T, and gave it to me for a present. When I came down, I thought I hated him because of that. But after Marvin, I knew I'd just hate anybody I tripped with, it's just part of the trip." She looked at the magazine in her lap. "You know, I think she could actually get that in her mouth. Marvin was bigger."

By the time we arrived at Jerry Lawson's house, the two had sobered up, and cleaned up spots of ice cream from their clothing that had escaped during the fits of giggles.

The neighborhood was nice. It had sidewalks, lawns, single family homes, some with two stories, most with one. I stood to the side of Lawson's door, and the two women stood in front of it as if they were selling Girl Scout cookies. I rang the bell, although we had certainly been announced automatically, and recorded. Doorbells are a courtesy.

We stood there for a while, and no action came from the house. Cat looked around for cameras, but really didn't expect to find them. She picked a likely spot and spoke to it anyway.

"Hi, we're Margaret Jackson's daughters, and her friend Joey at Lawrence Liquors said we might find her here." She pulled Joey's phone number out of her bra and read off the number. "Call Joey when you see this video, if you can help us find her. We came all the way out from Maryland to help her out with, well, she'll know, she sent us the message. Anyway, too bad we couldn't connect, Joey said you were a good guy, and Mom liked you."

We got back into the car. Cat called Joey, voice only, straight to messaging. "Hi, Joey honey, this is Cat, we met at the store a little bit ago and you gave me your number. I'm really careful who I give my number out to, and I don't know your friend Jerry Lawson, so when he wasn't at home, I told the house to have him call you. I hope that's OK, sweetie, you seemed like such a nice guy, I knew you wouldn't mind. Anyway, I'll call you real soon, so take a message from him for me if he calls, would you dear? And you can let me know when you get off work, too. Bye for now! See ya!"

"You don't think he'll see through that obvious manipulation attempt?" I said when she had disconnected.

"Guys love to be manipulated. It keeps their hopes up. And they love it when girls owe them favors," Cat explained.

I pondered this as I called Jacob. "No one answered the door at Jerry Lawson's place," I said. "We're heading over to the Bayside biotech park."

"I wouldn't recommend that," Jacob said. "We've spotted two heavily muscled men with October Nine prison tattoos hanging around the area. One watching the front door, one the back, but from a distance, trying not to be noticed. They have big bags with them, probably pretty well armed, and they look like they could break a guy in half with one hand. I'm bringing in Katie. She's cute and looks harmless, but she teaches classes in kick-ass at the Naval academy. We're buying her a job at the sandwich counter as a cover, she can see the front door from there. We're planting cameras for the rest of the perimeter."

"Still no sign of Jerry Lawson I take it," I said.

"That's right."

"We'll stay at least a mile away, then. But I'm going to have the car takes us close and then go back, and we'll check out any likely routes he takes to and from work. Maybe we'll get lucky and spot him at a bar or a diner."

"Doing your own legwork on this one?" Jacob said, one eyebrow a little higher than the other one.

"Stretching our legs, getting some air. We'll stay in touch." I disconnected.

Cat looked over at me. "You're looking for Dad, aren't you." It was not a question.

"I'd like to find Lawson before your father does. We don't know what plans he has for that gun."

We spent the afternoon cruising. Most of the route was highway, without much in the way of distractions or attractions. On some of the alternate routes were laundromats, grocery stores, quick charge stops, and other places where one or the other man might have stopped, but not stayed long. We found a small cafe, and stopped inside for some pie and a milkshake for Cat, but it was on one of the more unlikely routes. The waitress had never seen Jerry or Jonathan. Cat left her Joey's number, and we left a very large tip.

It was well after dark when we returned to the house. We were all tired, and I turned on the pool lights, took off my clothes, and stepped into one of the hot pools. I closed my eyes and rested my head back on the edge of the pool, bubble jets scrubbing my back and legs. I heard one of the women step to the pool and dip in a foot, then slide in next to me. I could smell Cat's hair as she rested her head on my shoulder. Becca slid into the water next, with an audible sigh of pleasure.

"We need to get one of these," she said to Cat. "This is heaven."

§

Chapter Seventeen

In the morning after breakfast, I called Jacob to let him know I was telling Sam about the location of what we all presumed was a lab where Jerry Lawson worked.

"He probably already knows," Jacob said. "We've noticed some police tails on our people. We haven't tried to lose them, but they are being very discreet and polite. They probably haven't made Katie yet, or the other two new guys, and I'm keeping those guys away from the lab just in case I need someone the cops aren't watching. But it's kind of nice having the cops around, just in case. We're running a profile on the October Nine people, to see if it helps predict their behavior, but so far what we're getting is that they aren't afraid to kill, and they don't much care if they go back to prison to recruit more followers. And that isn't all that helpful in preventing trouble. We don't have any leverage on them."

"I'll call Sam anyway. Courtesy and all. I'll pretend we haven't made his tails." I disconnected.

Sam looked like he hadn't slept a lot. "Hi J.T. Your nights still better than mine?"

I ignored the comment. "Jake has some people watching what may be a genetics lab in the biotech park over at Bayside. Some of the people on my watch list seem to work there. Flex time, but roughly ten to sixish. And they have come across some of your October Nine visitors, or at least a couple that fit the description."

"We have some sightings on the board in that area," Sam said, not admitting he'd been following Jacob's people. Neither of us was fooling anyone, but that was the game we played. "You might want to back off a little where those people are concerned. They aren't only shooting up natural testosterone, they're on NeoTest and

Hype and who knows what else, and they don't react rationally to a perceived threat. They're very easy to set off, and very dangerous."

"I'll pass that on to Jake. We're also missing Jerry Lawson, one of the guys on my list. He's been off Jake's radar for two days. He may know something about Margaret Jackson and Jason Mallory. Apparently, they hung out together."

Sam's lips got a bit tighter. "Mallory was on the wrong side of October Nine, as far as we can tell. And there are O9's sniffing around where Lawson worked. And Lawson is missing. We may be looking for a body, or maybe two, if Lawson and the Jackson woman were tight. For that matter, Jonathan Worthington has come back to where his ex-wife lives, and he's carrying a handgun. He may have found Lawson and Jackson, and not liked what he saw. We don't have anyone on Worthington. We're chasing muscle with tattoos pretty much exclusively these days. Are you and Jake still keeping tabs on him?"

I shook my head. "He's leaving a trail of tagged virus, so Jake is just using sniffers, when his people aren't too busy tailing other persons of interest. We could pick up the trail pretty quickly, but I doubt we have any information on his whereabouts for the last 18 hours or more. And that trail is going to peter out pretty soon if someone doesn't tag him again. And he's smart enough to buy new antivirals at the first sign of a sniffle. He's probably already figured out he's been tagged."

Sam looked disappointed. "You know one of the treatments for Hinshaw Barnes is AGP phosphate. He's not going to be all that rational himself. And he's armed, since AGP isn't on the list for a weapons check. Tread carefully there, J.T. He's sure to know he's pushing the life expectancy odds already. Whatever he's up to, he may not care a lot how dangerous life gets."

I nodded. "Good luck, Sam," I said. "Hope you sleep better soon."

"Yeah, fuck you too, asshole. Keep safe." He disconnected.

Cat and Becca were playing tennis, and I watched them from the upstairs window for a while. Becca didn't have Cat's strength or form, but the robot scorekeeper showed a tie match on the board. Cat seemed to be more interested in keeping the ball in play than in scoring. Both women seemed to be having fun.

A call came in from Jacob, and his face appeared on the screen. "Jerry Lawson just left the lab. Looks like he slept in his clothes, maybe more than one night. As soon as the O9 goons left, he was out and in his car. I have someone on Lawson, and it looks like the police are tailing the goons, so we're staying out of that one. Looks like Lawson's heading for home, maybe a hot shower."

I thought for a moment. "Let's see what he does when he gets Cat's message. It's good to know he's alive. If he contacts Cat, we might learn about Margaret Jackson's whereabouts. If he doesn't, that might also tell us something, although I don't know exactly what yet. He may have called the house and gotten the message before he left, in which case he might not contact Cat, since he might have done that from the lab already."

Jacob looked blank for a moment. "Or, he could know nothing at all about Margaret Jackson."

"He's our only lead at this point. Let's hope he's of some help, one way or another. Jackson may not want to contact Cat and Becca. We may have to tail him to her."

"We'll stay on him," Jacob said, and disconnected.

The tennis court was empty, so I went down to the gym to fill in Cat and Becca on the morning's phone calls. They were already in the shower, so I started to work the dumbbell rack while I waited for them to come out. I was halfway through the rack when they appeared, hair still wet, but dressed.

"It looks like Jerry Lawson has been spending nights at the lab," I said. "Perhaps avoiding the muscle that has been watching the place. They left for some reason, and he bolted out as soon as they were gone. Jacob has someone tailing him, but he's likely going home."

"About what time do we expect he'll get home?" Cat said.

"He may be there by now. Soon anyway, if he's going straight home."

"I'm just wondering when to call Joey to ask for messages."

"Give him some time. He may need to think about it for a while. He's afraid enough of the goons to spend two nights at the lab, sleeping in his clothes. He isn't going to feel really comfortable interacting with strangers."

"You have so little faith in my sweet talk," Cat said.

"Maybe I should have unbuttoned another button," Becca said, smirking.

"Hey Jack, if I got all the flawless genes, how come she got the big boobs?" Cat asked.

I knew better than to answer. I picked up the next dumbbell and resumed my workout, and Cat and Becca left the gym.

When I had finished and showered, I met them in the kitchen, where they were eating some kind of grilled sandwich. "We made you one," said Cat. "Grilled cheese, bacon and sauerkraut," she continued, pointing to my plate. The sandwich had much more than that on it. I sat down.

"We were just trying to work it all out," Cat said. "Mom hooks up with this guy Jason, who just happens to work at a place that has some clue to what Dad did when they screened me for Hinshaw Barnes in some Petri dish. Or she figured out something, and then found a guy to hook up with that could get her in."

Becca continued for her. "Then she steals something, and has to keep it cold, so she hides it in the freezer at work. Was that before, or after, someone slices up her new boyfriend? If he's sliced up because of her stealing something, why do they wait a month before stealing it back? If he's sliced up for some other reason, how does she get in to steal the thing later?"

Cat took up the narrative again. "This guy goes into the store, shoots the clerk, finds the stuff in the freezer, and heads off somewhere with it. He gets a couple miles, and then gets killed with chemical weapons. Was he stopped to meet someone? Was he where he wanted to end up already? Did he know the guy that killed him? Otherwise, why stop?"

Becca squeezed in when Cat took a breath. "So now there's this other guy, Jerry, who was friends with Mom and her boy toy, who is hiding from friends of that Roland guy that got maced. He's got to know what they are after, that's why he's hiding."

They both looked at me expectantly.

"The Chinese government is pushing hard on Sam and the police to do something about the October Nine people. They are afraid October Nine has some new biological weapon that can be used for global ethnic cleansing. I find the claims for such a weapon to be highly suspect, and most likely just propaganda to aid in recruiting. Nonetheless, there are October Nine people hanging around the lab that Lawson and Mallory worked at, and that is being funded quietly and privately. A Chinese government agent might have access to sophisticated binary toxins, but why would they use one on

Roland Drake? Why not just shoot him? Using a weapon no one else has access to is like signing a confession."

"They want people to know who did it? They don't care who knows?" Cat asked.

"The Chinese government may want people like October Nine to know. And the agent who carried out the execution may have immunity from prosecution, or at least from extradition," I said.

"And another thing," Becca said. "This guy Jerry has been hiding for two days. Mom hasn't been back to her rooftop in two days. What if this guy is hiding from Mom instead of the tattooed muscle freaks?"

Cat looked at her sister with a puzzled expression. "Of the two, I don't think Mom is the scarier one."

"I mean, what if they were together, and just split up? What if she was stalking him?"

I spoke to keep Cat from pressing her point. "At this point, we should consider all of the possibilities. We can narrow our hypotheses later when we have more information."

"I guess that means I should call Joey," Cat said, reluctantly.

She set the camera to show only her face, and made the call. Joey answered on the first ring.

"Hi Joey! First, let me apologize for using you as my personal answering service, but I really hate to give out my phone number to strange older men, you know what I mean? You're not mad at me, are you?"

"Huh? Oh, no, that's straight. I get it." He paused for a while, as if thinking was not something he was used to doing. "Um, I get off at six, if you want to drop by..."

"Did Jerry Lawson call you?" Cat said, ignoring the suggestion.

"Oh, yeah, that guy. Yeah, he gave me a number. Just a minute, let me see if I can find where I put that thing." The camera tried to track the top of his head as he bent down to sort through scraps of paper bags with notes on them. "Yeah, this one, I think. I should have put his name on it." He held the scribbled note up to the camera. There was a phone number and the words "crab night Sunday".

"Are you sure that's it?" Cat asked.

"Pretty sure, yeah."

"What does 'crab night Sunday' mean?" she asked.

"Oh, that. He said you have to say that when you call. Like some kind of password for his voicemail or something."

"If I call this number I won't get a seafood restaurant?" Cat asked.

Joey was stumped. "Huh? No, it's his personal phone. He didn't give his work number. Was I supposed to get his work number?"

"No, Joey, you did great. You're the best. If I find Mom by six, we'll drop by to say hi, OK? Thanks a lot! I'm gonna call this number right now. See you later, OK?"

"Uh, OK," Joey said, and Cat disconnected before he could think of something else to say.

She told the house to rewind, and stopped it when the image of the phone number came up. She had apparently forgotten that she could have asked me. She was about to place the call when Jacob called.

"You'll never guess who showed up out of nowhere when Jerry Lawson's car pulled into the driveway," he said.

"Mom!" Becca almost shouted.

"Close," Jacob said. "Jonathan Worthington. Neither of them spotted the tail, as far as we can tell. Looks like Mr. Worthington's been sleeping rough, keeping an eye on the house. There's a car parked with a good view of the street and the driveway. He walked up and looked into Lawson's car, and then walked across the street. He's trying to stay inconspicuous, but apparently the car is too hot on a day like this to stay inside, and he doesn't want to use up the battery on the air conditioning. It's one of those cheap rentals with the limited range."

"We were just about to place a call to Mr. Lawson. Or his answering service, he gave us a password to use," I said.

"Good, because he isn't answering the house phone. I'd recommend against setting up a meeting while Worthington is tailing him. And don't let on that he's being tailed at all. He may just skip out altogether. He's acting really skittish," Jacob said.

"Good thing you called when you did," I said. "A meeting is exactly what we had in mind."

"If you do decide to meet Lawson somewhere, make it more than 40 miles away. Worthington will have to recharge the rental, and you can lose the tail easily while he does."

"Clever. I guess it pays to have more than one car tailing at a time," I said.

"Tricks of the trade, Jack. Two or three cars also make it harder to spot the tail."

He disconnected, and Cat brought up the image of Lawson's number again. She called him.

The phone picked up on the first ring, in voice only mode, but no one greeted the call. There was some faint background noise, and what might have been breathing. Cat waited for a voice for a while before she realized what was expected of her. "Crab night Sunday" she said.

"You wanted to talk," came a quiet voice. "So, talk."

"Mr. L-" Cat started.

"No names!" came the voice quickly, shouting over her.

"Sorry," Cat said. There was a long pause before Cat realized she was expected to continue.

"We're looking for, um, a mutual acquaintance," she began. There was no sound from the other side of the conversation. She continued. "I was wondering if we could talk to you in person."

"Not going to happen," came the answer.

"Well then could I ask if you've seen, um, this person? Recently?" Cat said quickly, afraid he would hang up.

"What if I had?" came the answer.

"We want to talk to... this person," Cat said.

There was another pause. "And you have reason to believe this person would like to converse with you as well?"

"Oh yes, yes... This person would definitely want to converse with me."

There was another pause. "Call me again tomorrow. Each time you call, add a day to the code word. Say the code word you will use for tomorrow's call."

Cat looked up at me. "Crab night Monday," she said.

"Tomorrow. Not before noon." The phone disconnected.

Becca spoke first. "That guy sounds like he writes ransom notes for a living."

"He knows enough to be aware he's in danger," I said. "And, we now have reason to believe your mother is still alive."

"You thought she might be dead?" Becca said, horrified.

"So far, no one has tried to hide any bodies. So no, I didn't think she had been killed. But now we have reason to believe she is alive."

"You have a way of comforting without giving any comfort at all," Cat said.

"If he had any social skills, he might have a different nickname," Becca said.

I reflected a moment. "Your father seems to have some effective detective methods himself."

"He used to be pretty smart, at least when the meds were working. He makes a lot of money designing proteins," Cat said.

"Do you think he's been in contact with your mother? He knew to find Jerry Lawson," I said.

"You think she's been keeping him up to date on her love life? I really don't know what they say when she calls. Dad usually gets upset when she does, though. But it's probably because she's never sober when she calls. And she likes to fuck with his head, piss him off. She knows his buttons," Becca offered.

"I'm just trying to put him in place in the puzzle," I said. "We have so many interested parties, I'd like to figure out who he is aligned with. Is he working with the GenePharm people, with your mother, with the painted bigots, with the Chinese, or is he a party unto himself, with an agenda orthogonal to the others?"

"Mom said she knows what he did to Cat. That's illegal, right, what he did? Maybe he just wants to make sure she doesn't tell the police. He wouldn't hurt her, though." Becca looked over at her sister for support. "I'm sure he wouldn't hurt her."

Cat did not look so certain. "Maybe he came to save her."

"From Jerry Lawson?" asked Becca. "He'd hide the body, wouldn't he? He isn't like those muscle Nazis. He wouldn't want to advertise. What if he's killed her? What if he wants to kill us, so we don't find out?"

"She's alive," Cat said. "She has to be alive. Dad came to make sure she stays OK. Just like we did. We all want to help her. Jerry Lawson was her friend. Even he's trying to help her. She's going to be OK. We just have to find her." Cat stroked her sister's hair. As for me, I could not find fault with Becca's logic.

"How about a change of scenery?" I asked. "Are you up for a drive down the coast?"

The suggestion met with approval. We picked the limousine.

The big car wound through the mountain road between the redwoods and firs, the early afternoon sun flashing through the trees. We opened the large sunroof and reclined the seats, and looked up at the trees as they flowed by. Becca took off her shoes and rested her feet out the open window in the wind. Our seats faced each other, with Cat by my side, and Becca across from us. For a while we sat silent, listening to the wind roar through the open windows, Becca's hair blown back.

When we reached the ridge top, we could see the blanket of clouds hiding the ocean. After another ten minutes or so, we were inside those clouds, and the air got cooler. Becca pulled her feet in, and we raised the windows. Driving through the cloud infused woods in the quiet, the drive took on a dreamy aspect, like a trip through a fairy tale.

"Back home, the weather is so humid and hot," Cat said. "But here, everything is cool and green. You'd have thought it was summer already on the other side of the mountains, it's so warm. But here, it's actually crisp."

We came out from beneath the clouds, and the Pacific stretched out forever, first on one side of the car and then on the other, as we glided down the mountain. Once on the flat coast, we lost sight of it in the trees again, until we came out onto the coast highway, and drove along the high cliffs above the breakers. The sun occasionally broke through the clouds that hugged the coastline, and we could see clear blue skies out to sea.

Driving down the coast put all the worries of the city behind us, and the talk turned to favorite vacations, and places the two women wanted to see someday.

We reached the beach house before sunset. The big gates opened for the car, and we drove around the back, past pine trees sculpted by the wind. The back of the house was low and unassuming, paneled in wood bleached by sun and salt breezes. Inside, the view opened onto a three-story wall of glass facing the ocean, as the house grew down the side of the hill towards the cliffs. We walked down the wide stairs to the middle level, where the balcony looked over the floor below.

"This is amazing," Cat said, taking in the view of the ocean, but also of the rest of the huge open house.

"Thanks," I said. "I designed this one myself."

I had phoned ahead, and dinner was waiting for us in the dining room.

"Maria," I said, as we walked into the room, "This is Cat," I said, nodding to the blonde who had attached herself to my hip, "and this is Becca. Ladies, this is Maria, who takes care of Windcall for me, and washes the salt spray off of all those windows every day."

"Don't listen to him. There's a little robot thing that does that. I spend most of my time in the garden."

"There are only three plates," I said. "You're not planning to join us for dinner?"

Her eyes brightened, and she wiggled her hips as she passed by me. "I have a date," she said, and giggled. "He's taking me out to the La Boheme."

"Is this your professor friend? He's going to spend his whole paycheck wining and dining you. You'd better be nice to him to-night."

She winked at me. "Leave the dishes on the table, I'll be back in the morning to do the cleaning up." With that, she went upstairs to-wards the garage, and we saw nothing of her after that.

By dessert, the sun was setting, and the clouds were painted in or-anges and reds all along the horizon. Becca had gone to explore the house, and Cat and I were relaxing in the deep soft sofa facing the sunset.

Cat rested her head on my shoulder. "It's going to be quite a let-down to go back to the dorms after all of this," she said.

"You have what, three weeks left of school? Then you can come back, maybe start looking for where you want to do your graduate work. Stanford's pretty close to Dad's house, and Berkeley's nice, or you can come down here to Santa Cruz."

"Sam said not to expect a long relationship."

"Sam doesn't know you well yet, or he would know better. Give him some time, he'll see."

"What's your track record? Don't you drive them all away within a week?"

"I didn't say he was stupid. I said he didn't know *you*."

"Don't mess with me, Jack. I can handle it if you're not serious, but if I trust you, and you fuck it up... Well, Becca's not the only one who's fragile."

"It's been twelve days. That's long enough for me to know what I'm doing. But I understand that it isn't enough time to let you trust me. If you want to take your time, we have all the time in the world. I'm not afraid of you running away." I brushed a strand of hair from her face, and kissed her on the forehead.

"Hey, Cat!" came a shout from above. "I found *my* bedroom. There's a swimming pool that's half inside the house and half out-side, and you can swim under the glass to get to the other side. And one of those hot pools right inside the bedroom. And all the boats out on the water can see me naked in the shower if they have bin-oculars, the whole shower wall is clear glass. Come check it out!"

"Be sure to push the button to cover the outside pool at night, or you might have raccoons in your bed in the morning," I called out.

"Rag, that would be so straight! I love raccoons!" Becca shouted, still a level above and four doors down.

"She's obviously not slept with one yet," I murmured to Cat. We got up, and joined Becca, who acted as tour guide through the rest of the house.

Later that night, after playing together in the hot shower and then resuming in the big bed, Cat again laid her head on my shoulder and I dimmed the lights. "I think maybe I trust you already," she said.

"You'll have three weeks in a dorm room to see if you miss me," I said.

"What about Becca? She'll be thousands of miles away."

"Did I mention I have a private jet?" I asked.

"Maybe she could transfer. Come out west and go to school nearby."

"At some point you're going to have to stop protecting her and let her grow up by herself."

"And when that time comes, I'm sure she'll be ready. But for a while you're stuck with a two-fer."

"An adolescent's dream come true," I said.

"She likes it when you stare at her tits," Cat said.

"I'm glad we're both having fun, then," I said.

"I'm glad you didn't screw her that first night. Everything would be different."

"I like that things aren't different."

"Me too," she said, and snuggled closer, kissing the back of my neck. After a few minutes, her breathing slowed, and we both fell asleep.

I awoke to the smells of breakfast. Cat's head was still resting on my shoulder, and as I moved, she woke and stretched. "Smells good," she said sleepily.

Cleaned up and dressed, we went downstairs to find Becca sitting in the big kitchen, wrapped in a bathrobe, her hair still wet. Maria was busy at the stove.

"That pool is amazing. Like swimming in a cloud," Becca said.

"That's because it's full of pure demineralized water," Maria said. "This whole place is built on top of the desalination plant. You can't get permits to build on the coast anymore, so Jack bid for the job of building the desalination plant, and put the house on top of it. The water in the pool is used for all the landscaping, so it is constantly flushing out."

"It also keeps deposits from forming on the glass wall," I said.

Becca looked up at Maria. "I want to apologize. I was exploring last night, and I went into your room. I didn't know, and I didn't want to invade, so I left right away."

"No problem," Maria said. "But you should go back in and check out the trophy wall."

I said nothing. Maria wanted to fill the house with framed awards and articles from architecture magazines, but I vetoed that. I'll do my own bragging. But what she does in her own suite is her own business. The awards she *should* be proud of are the landscaping awards, which she earned by herself. But instead, her favorite is the poetic fluff piece from AD, the year the design awards came out. "Isolated, yet invitingly open, balanced on the edge of a cliff, yet looking out to the horizon, self-sufficient and bold, there is much of Jack Wright in everything he creates." I suspect she had a hand in crafting that particular line, just to get back at me for all the arguments we had during the construction. Her version would have read *unbalanced* though.

Becca ran her fingers though her wet hair. "Why did you need to build another house, when you only live in the one your father built?"

Maria laughed. "I can answer that one!" I gave her a cold eye, but she continued anyway. "It was to show his sister-in-law how to do it right. He doesn't do anything unless there's something to win."

Cat grinned at this, and looked at me with a raised eyebrow. I shrugged.

We ate breakfast. Maria makes her living as a landscape architect, but she is also an excellent cook, and loves to show off. She lives in the house mostly to show off her talents to prospective customers, but also because even the best landscape architect could not afford to live in a place like Windcall, and I need someone to live in it to keep it maintained. We had both put enormous effort into the design of the whole effect, and she had earned the right to live there.

After breakfast, Cat insisted on a dip in the pool, but we made it quick, since I wanted to be back in the city before noon, in case the phone call to Lawson delivered a face-to-face meeting.

We took the much faster inland route home. Fewer trees, straighter roads, even through the mountains, but less relaxing and less interesting.

Cat sat with her seat turned towards me, her feet stretched across my lap. "What are the odds that Mr. 'Help help the paranoids are after me' actually knows where Mom is? And will tell us?"

"In this case, I think the paranoids are actually after him," I said. "But to answer your question, consider this: of all the people we know who your mother might have gone to for help, he is the only one who has not denied seeing her recently."

"And he's been missing for about the same amount of time Mom has," said Becca. "I find that really suspicious."

"Or hopeful," I said. Becca looked down at my feet, then back up.

"So why *are* the paranoids after him?" Cat said.

"We're assuming October Nine wants him, or wants him dead. That is because we, or at least I, think that October Nine killed Jason Mallory, presumably to find what your mother hid in the freezer. Mallory and your mother likely stole it from the lab where Lawson and Mallory worked. However, it is possible that Lawson is who they stole it from, and he arranged to kill Mallory, and is now looking for your mother, or already has her and is collecting anyone that she might have talked to about something he wants kept secret. In that case, he would be hiding from whoever killed Roland Drake, who I suspect is a member of October Nine."

"Jack," said Cat, "you make everything seem so tangled up. What do we need to do to sort out who is connected to whom?"

"We find out who he is afraid of. If there were only two parties involved, it would be simple. He was staying in the lab, and only left when the goons left. Thus, he's afraid of October Nine, not in cahoots with them. However, we don't know who killed Roland Drake. If it was the people in the lab, then there are only two parties, and it's simple. But I don't think the lab folks would have used illegal exotic military nerve agents. They'd have just bought guns and shot him. Thus, there are three parties, and he is hiding from one of the two outside the lab. The obvious one is October Nine, because he left when they left. But since we don't know who killed Roland Drake, we don't know if that party also left at the same time."

"I just wish he'd tell us where Mom is, so we could get her and leave all this shit behind," Becca said.

"At which point, we'd know why your father was here. If all three of you were back in Maryland, then he'd return to be with you if he was here to find her. If he is here to erase evidence of how Cat was conceived, then he would stay to finish that."

"How could he erase the evidence?" Becca asked.

"If it was some record of his involvement, he may try to erase computer files and any off-site backups. Or he could just be trying to help the people he used to work with to patch a leak. Your mother is the most likely leak, although Jerry Lawson might also need to be convinced to keep quiet."

"But if Mom is the leak, and she's in Maryland, then he comes back just as if he was only after her," Cat said.

"But your mother will know his reasons for coming back," I pointed out.

Cat changed the subject. "So, if this lab has been running for 25 years, there might be lots of people like me running around. People with all the bad genes replaced with the good stuff. Who would the customers be, and which party are they with?"

I considered this. "I would imagine October Nine might be interested in a eugenics program. However, they don't really strike me as family men. They have access to funds, but not the kind of funds required to run a lab like that for 25 years. Also, they haven't been around for 25 years. We're likely looking for a class of people who need secrecy, need genetic manipulation, and have money. The question is, would someone in that class have access to military nerve agents, and a reason to use them on Roland Drake instead of just shooting him."

"I wonder how much mom knows?" Cat said. "She might be able to tell us. But if she knows too much, she might be in danger no matter where she goes."

"Or she might be dead," Becca said in a low tone.

"If she's dead, we go home and let Sam find out who the bad guys are," Cat said. "But until we know she's dead, we assume she's not, and we try to find her."

It was easy to tell who had the optimism genes.

When we got home, there was a message waiting from Jacob. Apparently, it was not important enough to call me personally in the car.

"Just a heads-up," Jacob began. "Our boy Jonathan Worthington managed to tail Lawson all the way to the biotech park. But Lawson never got out of the car. We think he made one of the cars the October Nine idiots are using. They don't switch cars, and they don't switch who's watching the lab, so it's easy to keep track of them. It's unlikely he was seen, but Worthington followed him back home, and then came back to the park and circled around for hours. He's sure to be on their suspicious list by now. So, if you run into our boy somewhere, be prepared to see some muscled goons hanging around."

I looked over at Cat. "It is possible that your father does not know about October Nine, or the danger they pose. He may think he's only dealing with GenePharm. He's behaving too recklessly to be aware of the trouble he could get into."

"If his meds aren't working anymore, he might not care," Becca said. "He knows he doesn't have a lot of time to do whatever he wants to do. And without the meds, his thinking is going to be messed up anyway."

"Nonetheless, I think I'll have Jacob leave a message on his phone, with some data on October Nine, some photos of the guys hanging around the lab, and the report on Jason Mallory's unfortunate circumstances. That will double as a reminder that he has someone watching over his shoulder, too. Keep him a little sharper, maybe save him an accident," I said, looking at Becca.

We waited until noon, and then placed the call to Jerry Lawson.

Cat did the speaking, the camera focused on her face. "Crab night Monday." she said, and waited.

"Punctual," Lawson said, in a low voice.

"I am very anxious to speak with my mother," Cat replied.

"There's been a snag," he said. "Not unexpected. But I am unable at the moment to get a message to her. There's a certain amount of risk involved for me, personally. But I expect to be seeing her soon."

"Can you tell me where she is?" Cat asked.

"Why would I do that? I don't know you. If she wants to contact you, that's her business. But I'm not giving out anything to strangers just for asking. I'll let her know you want to talk, she'll see the video, she can decide whether she wants you to know where she is. For the moment, the fewer people who know where she is, the safer she is."

"Is she in danger?" Cat asked.

"What is this, a fishing expedition? I just said I don't give out information."

Cat looked over at me, questioningly. I pantomimed showing all my cards on the table.

"Let me generate some trust," she said, still watching my face intently. I nodded encouragement. "I'll tell you what we know. You decide after that how much or how little you want to share. Mom worked at Lawrence Liquors, and after someone named Roland Drake shot the night clerk and stole something from the freezer in a small paper bag, she has gone missing. Roland Drake was killed not far from the store by means of some military nerve toxin, and apparently robbed of the small paper bag. Roland Drake appears to have been associated with a neo-Nazi group called October Nine, who are implicated in the torture and murder of Jason Mallory, a known associate of both you and my mother. This same group has been hanging around the place where you and Mallory work, or worked, together. We have been interviewed by the police, which is where we learned much of this information."

Cat waited for a reply. Lawson was apparently thinking all of this over. "Where is the sample that Drake took now?" he said, after the pause.

Cat looked over at me. I gave an encouraging nod. "If you don't have it, and your co-workers don't have it, then I would assume there is a third party, not connected to you or to October Nine, who killed Roland Drake and now has the bag."

"You say Drake was killed with some military toxin. Whose military would that be?" Lawson asked in a quiet voice.

"The police don't know. Nobody is supposed to have that stuff, there are treaties against it," Cat said.

"Well, I guess it's nice to have people with means helping us with our vermin problems. However, I don't like the idea of trading the vermin we know for some more effective vermin." Lawson paused again. Cat, not wanting the conversation to end, quickly stepped in.

"What do those guys want with you? What does my mom have to do with any of this?"

"I'm not going to discuss these things over the phone. This has gone on long enough as it is. Tomorrow, not before noon," he said, and disconnected.

"Shit," Becca said. "That was useless. We could have stayed at the beach."

Cat looked over at me. "If we believe him, then there's someone we don't know who likes to rid the world of people like Roland Drake."

"And the bag contained a sample of something that had to be kept frozen," I said. "Not an object, or a shipment, or a tool, but a sample."

"And he doesn't know who killed Drake," Becca said, revising her earlier opinion.

"He also didn't jump to correct you about working with Mallory, knowing your mother, or goons hanging around his place of business. Not that he would, but he might have," I said.

"And he is concerned about where the sample is now," Cat said.

"Or who has it. Either he wants it back for its intrinsic value, or for its value as evidence against him, or for what someone might do with it. Not a lot of information, but more than we had this morning," I said. "I should go upstairs and get some work done."

"I'll be in the media room," Becca said. "I'm thinking about changing my major to architecture. I'm going to see if the net can talk me out of it."

Cat, my new shadow, followed me upstairs.

"You left some things out of your speech to Lawson," I said. "That's not the best way to generate trust."

"You mean about Dad? I can't tell him my father is following him around. Not when we suspect he might be a killer. And I don't think I want Mom to know Dad's here, anyway. That would complicate a whole bunch of things."

"Which brings me to something else you left out. You've never lied to me, in almost two weeks. That is highly unusual, unprecedented, in fact. But you left out why your mother really left."

Cat looked around the room. "You really ought to have a chair or a couch in here," she said, and let herself down onto the carpet, resting on one elbow to look up at me.

I touched the screen and brought up a display of data graphs, and began working. On a second screen, I added the information we'd just received from Lawson, and some of my own inferences to the searches currently in progress. Cat lay back with her hands under her head and watched me in silence for several minutes.

"I was almost five years old," she said. "Becca was a little over a year. I used to love taking care of her, she was my real live baby doll. I could change her. I could warm up the formula and test it on my lip to make sure it wasn't too hot. I could heat up her baby food in the microwave, it had a special button for that. Mom was functional most of the time. She always had a glass with ice in it, and if it was ever empty, it got refilled right away."

She paused, remembering, or thinking about how she was going to tell the story.

"She'd take naps. Sometimes in the morning, sometimes in the afternoon. Sometimes Dad would come home while she was asleep and he'd get angry for a while, cleaning up the house, banging things around, but he never yelled at her, he'd just pick her up off the couch or off the floor and carry her into bed. Sometimes she'd wake up, but not usually."

I touched the screen, made some adjustments to the trading programs. Cat rolled onto her side, her elbow on the carpet, hand propping up her head.

"Mom was cooking something for us for lunch. I was playing with Bec, she was frying something at the stove, drinking from the bottle instead of the glass of ice. Then she sort-of just stood there, not moving, looking out the window. When she fell down, the bottle fell onto the stove."

I turned around to look down at Cat.

"I tried to get her to wake up. Her nose was bleeding and I got blood all over my dress. The kitchen started to stink, and I tried to put the fire out by filling a glass of water from the sink, but after a few glasses it was too hot to get to the sink anymore. I couldn't pull Mom out of the kitchen. I got her phone and pushed the speed dial button for Dad. He told me to get Bec and go next door and tell them what was happening. Mr. Olson came over and got Mom out, but he burned his hands getting her shoes off. They were on fire and the rubber smelled really bad. The fire trucks came, and then Dad got home, and we lived in an apartment while the workers fixed the house."

Cat sounded like the five-year-old who had lived through that experience. Her voice changed back to the adult Cat as she continued.

"Mom tried to quit. There were no bottles in the apartment. She'd go to meetings, every day at first. She had some pills she was supposed to take, and Dad was supposed to make sure she took them. We had Nancy stay with us when Dad was at work. She was nice, but Mom hated her. Mom would go out to meetings, or she would just go out, and sometimes she'd come back smelling like licorice and hiding in her room. She cried a lot. Then one day, she cried all day, and kissed me and Bec a lot, and packed a suitcase and she didn't come home. Dad cried a lot when he read the letter she wrote. When the house was all fixed up, Dad sold it, and bought a house close to work, so he could come home to have lunch with us every day."

Cat stopped talking, and played with a strand of hair that had fallen across her face. I sat down on the floor next to her.

"The new house was too far for Nancy, so we got a new babysitter. We had a lot of babysitters and nannies for a while. But I always took care of Becca, got her ready for school, helped Dad make breakfast, helped her with her homework. When I was about twelve, the last nanny had to move away, and I just took over. I'd call Dad every couple of hours, to check in. I became the mom."

Cat moved over to put her head in my lap. "Mom would call. Sometimes it would be months between calls, sometimes she'd call twice in the same week. She almost always cried. Sometimes she was sloppy drunk, sometimes she was almost a normal person. Sometimes if Dad was home, she'd just hang up. Other times she'd ask him how things were going. We'd get presents at Christmas and on our birthdays. Sometimes late, sometimes weeks ahead, and we'd save the presents, all wrapped up, until the right time. Sometimes they were really nice presents, some trendy doll or game that every kid had to have that year. Sometimes they were really weird, like socks that we'd never dare wear to school, or this funny hat that Becca kept on top of the lamp by her bed for years. She loved that funny hat."

Cat wiped tears from her eyes. "We need to find Mom. We have to make sure those fuckers don't hurt her."

She stood up, and sniffed, and wiped her eyes again. She looked at me as I stood up. "You left out a bunch of shit too, you know," she said. "You finish up here, I'm going to go for a swim or something."

I spent another hour working on trading programs, selling some models of mining futures, but the part of my brain that came up with flashes of genius was otherwise occupied. Finally, I gave up trying to make money and called Jacob.

"Jake," I said, using the name I usually used only with Sam. "How difficult would it be to fake a trash pickup, and get the dumpster from the lab over to someone who can pick through it looking for something? Something that looks legitimate, so no suspicions are aroused by any of the various groups watching the place."

"Get a trash truck on short notice? That might be difficult. Maybe we could rent a truck and buy a new dumpster, and just swap them. We could throw up some magnetic signs with the right logos on them. I think I could get that done. What are we looking for?"

"Bottles of Southern Comfort. Disposable cups and plasticware, anything that someone camping out in the lab might have left some DNA on."

"You think she's in the lab?" Jacob asked.

"It's one of the places we haven't looked yet," I said. "Get DNA barcodes for whatever you find, and send them to me. I have the codes for her daughters, we'll know if she's been there if they compare."

"There's a delivery guy that makes runs twice a day. I'll see if we can buy a list of items from him," Jacob said. "But only if I think we can trust him not to tip off the wrong people."

I nodded, and he disconnected.

I called Sam.

"Hi J.T. Got something for me?" he said. He was in his office, and I could hear dull chatter from the other desks at the station.

"We talked with Lawson. He wanted to know where the sample was that was in the bag at the liquor store. He was interested to know what killed Roland Drake. So, he doesn't have the bag, and he doesn't know who killed Drake. We have a third party."

"And you believe this?" he asked.

"It was voice only, so I didn't get a lot of tells. But it was self-consistent, no stress at the wrong places, so yeah, I believe it," I said.

"Any idea who this third party might be?" Sam asked.

"I'd look for someone who doesn't like October Nine, and has access to proscribed military nerve agents, and who has political clout they can use to put pressure on local police forces," I said.

"Shit," came Sam's answer. "Are those your guys following consulate employees around?"

"Could be. I'd be surprised if there weren't several interested parties following them."

"That's as close to an admission as I'm going to get from you on a recorded line. Don't cause trouble for me, J.T. But keep me informed, or you could end up as a defendant."

"When have I ever let you down, Sammy?"

"I'm keeping a list. Had to get a bigger notebook for it, but I've got most of them down."

I smiled and reached to disconnect. Sam stopped me with a glance. "You'll want to know your hunch was right. Roland Drake was October Nine. Had some tats removed, but shared cells with four of them at different times. We traced some funds transfers, and he's been seen with other October Nine members."

"Good to know," I said. "But I've been pretty sure of that for a while. Just nothing that would make it to court."

"Be careful, J.T., these are not nice kitties."

"You too, Sam." I disconnected.

I stood in front of the big screens for a few minutes, reflecting. I brought up the tapes of all my sessions with four different psychologists, their notes, their summaries, their lists of important scenes in the video data. There it all was, the life of John Thomas Wright, Jack to his acquaintances, asshole to his friends. The history of what went wrong with Wright. I placed a memory chip into the slot, and loaded it with all I had ever told anyone about what it is to be Jack Wright. Such a small thing, the story of a life, it all fits into something the size of a fingernail, with room for the rest of the story, even considering the longevity genes and the best medical help money can buy.

"Open the safe," I said to the house, and the wood paneled wall of the room slid back, revealing the concrete and steel room Dad had built into his study. Dad loved secret rooms and hidden doors, so the house was full of them. This is one of the few I actually used occasionally. I walked into the safe, and opened Mom's big jewelry case. The locket hung where it had since Dad put it away. I took it off the hook and opened it. A picture of four people looked back at me. Two young adults, and two young children, smiling real smiles, all piled into the same large chair, arms around everyone. I had that same picture, life sized, in the main room downstairs. I carefully removed the photograph, and placed it in the drawer where her wedding ring rested. I put the memory chip inside the locket, closed it back up, and slipped it into my shirt pocket.

I closed the jewel case and walked out of the safe. The house quietly closed the safe door, and I went downstairs. The sun was almost touching the horizon, and there was no one out by the pool. The media room was quiet, the kitchen was empty. I found Becca and Cat upstairs to the observatory, sitting on the floor, backs against the wall, watching the sunset. Cat patted the floor next to her. I sat down.

"No clouds," said Becca. "Sunsets are better with clouds."

The ridge to the west of us hid the ocean, and the sun would slip below it before full sunset, and the backlit trees would glow on the ridgetop. For now, the sun was just reddening, and had not touched the ridge.

I pulled the locket out and opened Cat's hand, then slowly placed the locket in her palm, letting the chain coil around it. She took it in both hands to open it, and saw the memory chip inside.

"Let me know if I left anything out," I said.

She closed the locket slowly, and examined the simple case.

"Pretty," Becca said, reaching for the clasp to help Cat put it on. Cat looked up at me, one eyebrow raised in a question, but said nothing. The chain around her neck, she held the locket in one hand, and my hand in the other. We watched the sun set.

After a quiet dinner, Becca retired to the media room, and Cat went upstairs to the bedroom. I made one more check of the search results, and stayed a few minutes more in the upstairs study to dictate a message to Jacob. I joined Cat in the bedroom a few minutes later. She was standing by one of the data screens, wearing only the locket. I stood quietly, enjoying the magnificent view as she scanned the data on the screen.

"Do you really want me to see all of this?" she asked.

"As much as you like. I've given it to four different total strangers so far, I see no reason not to share it with you."

"I guess I shouldn't be surprised that it's so well organized," she said. She pulled the chip from the reader and placed it back in the locket. She walked over to me and put her hands behind my neck. "There are things you might tell a psychiatrist that you would never tell a lover," she said, kissing me on the chest.

I lifted her chin and kissed her on the lips, gently at first. When we came up for air, I whispered in her ear. "I wouldn't know, I've never had a lover before."

§

Chapter Eighteen

Cat was already up and out somewhere when I awoke in the morning. It was late, but not too late, and I went downstairs to the gym for my workout. Cat wasn't there. I ran uphill on the treadmill, worked myself to exhaustion on machines I hadn't touched in months, and did the full rack of dumbbells, although I had to rest twice while working the rack, to catch my breath and let the lactic acid drain from the muscles in my arms. I could see Becca swimming laps alone in the pool. Having no excuse to stay in the gym any longer, I showered and dressed, and went in to the kitchen. Cat was not there.

There was no sound from the media room. The house seemed completely empty. I went upstairs to the study, and pulled up the morning's messages. There were several, but one from Jacob received first priority. "Picked up the trash, and talked to the delivery guy. Got two different pictures of what's going on in there. Call me."

My muscles were still trembling, especially my legs, and I was reconsidering having chairs in the study. I called Jacob.

"Hey there, Jack! Had a nice discussion with the delivery guy. Turns out he has a hobby, restoring old gasoline motorcycles. Very happy to take that old thing off your hands. Good thing we could find one on such short notice, too. Surprising how expensive those are, some sort of collector's item. Anyway, the lab's been getting daily deliveries for almost two weeks now, quite unusual he says, they used to only get office supplies every couple of weeks. Now it's all kinds of foodstuffs and sundries, including, you're going to love this, a fifth of Southern Comfort every day. How about that?"

"So. She *is* there," I said.

"Maybe not. Here's where it gets weird. We swapped the dumpster with a brand new one. You know how hard it is to get those things on a same day basis? We had guys going through the trash, drew lots on who got that job, not fun at all. The dumpster is emptied every Saturday, so there's six days worth of trash in there, pretty ripe. Guess what we found?"

"Six bottles of Southern Comfort," I said.

"Well, yes, but here's the kicker. They were never opened. Tax stamp still in place. A couple had stains from coffee grounds on them, but aside from that, they could go right back on the shelf. Terry said he earned them, so if you don't need them, I'm letting him have them. He's the one who drew the short straw."

"They expected someone to notice the deliveries, and wanted them to think she was at the lab, when she's somewhere else? That sounds really farfetched. These aren't chess players. They keep things simple. Something else is going on," I said, uncertainly. I'd let this percolate through the back of my mind for a while.

"There's no point taking DNA from the bottles, but we did barcode all of the plasticware, straws, paper cups, soda cans and anything else that might have touched lips. I'll send you the codes."

"Thanks. I can run a comparison in a few minutes and we'll know if she's eaten there this week. Not nearly as definitive as if the bottles had been empty, but you take what you get," I said. "How about Lawson, has he been around?"

"He came by, spotted the goons, then went home by the long way," Jacob said. "Really long way, like 45 miles. Looks like he's figured out that the goons are renting short range vehicles. Not that they saw him. Doesn't look like he spotted any of our tails. He's sharp, but no pro."

"Any signs that the GenePharm folks are negotiating with October Nine? This standoff has been going on for days now, like a siege. GenePharm could have called in the police anytime, so I presume they have something they don't want the police to see. Any sign they've spotted Sam's people?"

"All the network traffic to the building is encrypted. We're staying legal on this, so we haven't even recorded any of it, let alone send it out for decryption. We don't have that kind of time, anyway. As for the cops, your old pal Detective Johnson is playing janitor, has his hardware hidden under soapy water in his mop bucket. There's a marked car that makes passes through the park at six pm every day, and they have four undercovers rotating shifts at odd times. The police have the whole place staked out with video, and there are three marked cars that never get more than a minute away. The goons fade at six o'clock, but they stay in the video, and they don't hide from the unmarked cars."

"I take it Lawson doesn't know he can enter at six o'clock without getting noticed," I said.

"That, or he's afraid of the cops," Jacob said. The screen made a small click, indicating that the DNA barcode data had arrived. Jacob watched me as I set up the comparison with Becca's sequence. We had Becca's entire sequence, done with state-of-the-art equipment and a large sample size. The barcode data was much less complete, a sampling from a marker chip. This made the comparison go faster, and the results would come up in a minute or two.

"He does seem to be rather aware of his predicament," I said, continuing the train of thought. "His caution may be overplayed, but maybe that helps him sleep. We don't know how close he was to Mallory, but I'm sure he doesn't want that to happen to him as well. But something is keeping him from going to the police. Anyone in fear of his life might be expected to worry less about a little jail time."

Jacob smiled. "Unless he expected to share that jail with some tattooed muscle that had an agenda."

"Something tells me there's more to it than that. Maybe he's also
protecting someone else. Or there's some loyalty to his GenePharm
pals. The third party in all of this makes it all the more complicated. We don't think Lawson knows who killed Roland Drake.
There seemed to be genuine surprise at that, and with the method.
But he could know there is a third party by some other means. Perhaps Lawson's been contacted," I said.

"I can tell you're eager to have a personal chat with Lawson," Jacob
said. In the middle of his sentence, there was a short tone, and the
barcode results came up.

"You said Stanley Johnson was playing janitor at the park," I said.
"I'll bet a janitor can get us a sample of trash from your new dumpster. Margaret Jackson has eaten at least one meal in the lab in the
last six days. If we get a positive hit on today's trash, we'll know
she's still there. He won't need a warrant for that, will he?" I asked.

"If he wants to use it in court, he'll want to be safe. But he can get
a warrant and come back for another sample if it comes to that,"
Jacob said.

"I'm going to make a call to Sam," I said. "We haven't been dumpster diving since we were kids."

I disconnected, and went downstairs to find Cat and Becca. Becca
was still out by the pool, sunning herself, wearing nothing but her
diamond ankle bracelet. She smiled as I took in the view apprecia-
tively. "Have you seen Cat?" I asked. "I have news for both of you."

"She's been hiding in the room at the end of the hall, going through
that stuff you gave her. She locked the door and wouldn't let me
in. Are we keeping secrets now?" Becca seemed more amused than
upset.

"I'm sure she'll share with her sister when she's done. Or at least paraphrase. It's up to her. You can ask me anything you like, and it's highly unlikely I would keep anything from you, at least as far as it pertains to me. But ask yourself — if you were reading someone's diary, wouldn't you want to do that alone, at least the first time?"

"You gave her your diary?" Becca asked, dubious.

"In a sense," I said. "You can ask her. Or wait until she shares." I pulled up a lawn chair and sat down across from her.

"You like her a lot, don't you," Becca said, making it a statement, not a question.

"Yes. I come to judgments about people quickly, and while that sounds like a bad thing, it rarely fails me. I like to think they are accurate assessments, and future interactions rarely bring forth evidence to the contrary. I've never met anyone like your sister. She's very special."

"Because of her genes?" Becca asked.

"In spite of her genes," I said.

"Doctor Garret says I don't really hate the people I trip with. He says I hate the part of me that needed to trip."

"He's a smart fellow, but some of the people you tripped with probably deserve your hostility," I said.

"But not you," Becca said.

"Perhaps you haven't been talking to very many people about me," I said.

"But I have. All the people you've introduced me to. Sometimes we talk until late at night. Yes, they all say you're an asshole. But they say it like it's a good thing, like they'd rather you were mean to them than, well, than not ever meeting you. It's like an honor or something, like you point out what they need to fix, and you don't accept excuses, and you don't care if it hurts. But when it hurts, they know it's real, and they can see how to fix it." Becca studied my face as she spoke.

"You've been talking to the people who still talk to me. There are lots more who never want to see me again. Not all of what's wrong with people can be fixed, and something in me can't tolerate broken people. It's like static on a radio, so irritating I have to tune to a different station, or turn it off. Being polite is just not an option, it just lets them hang around longer. The fastest way to get rid of them is to let them know just what bothers me. If some people benefit from that, that's fine with me. Most don't." I shifted in my chair. Lawn chairs have a habit of becoming uncomfortable, no matter how expensive they are.

"I could talk to you about anything, couldn't I, and you'd tell me exactly what you think," Becca said.

"Yes. So be very careful what you ask," I said.

She paused, thinking about that.

"Do you think I'm pretty?" she asked.

"Yes," I said without any hesitation.

"That first night, did you want to..."

"Yes," I said.

"But you didn't," Becca said, studying my face. "You lied to me then. Why?"

"You were lying to me. You didn't love me, the drug loved me. I was looking for sex. You were looking for someone to hate in the morning. What we got instead was better for both of us."

"You didn't take advantage. I think that's what made Cat want to know you, at first."

"I wish I could say I'd planned that," I said.

Becca stood up and stretched. "You said you had news."

"Let's go find Cat," I said. Becca picked up her towel and wrapped it around her, and we went inside.

At the door at the end of the hall, we stopped, and I knocked, calling out "Come on out, there's new news."

After a moment, the door opened, and Cat came out. "Isn't that redundant?" she said.

"Your mother has been in the lab sometime in the last six days," I said. "She's eaten a meal there, and she may still be there. We'll know after we pick through the trash tomorrow."

"So then, let's get our butts over there and talk to her," Cat said.

"And if she's being held there against her will?" I asked.

"We go in with the cops. Get her out of there," Cat insisted.

"And if she's there of her own free will, participating in something illegal?" I pressed.

"Shit, what do *you* think we should do, smart-ass?" Cat said, exasperated.

"Nothing rash, nothing sudden. There are a few pieces to the puzzle to put together first. Once we know the situation, we can plan the proper approach. First, we use Lawson. He doesn't know that the October Nine guys who are watching the lab go into hiding at six when the squad car makes its rounds. We can let him know that, and he can get inside. If your mother is still there, he can tell her about you and your sister, and if she's free to go, she can leave the following evening at six. Or she can invite us in for a chat. We can come and go as we please. We can arrange for the police to be visible any time we like." I tried to be soothing and rational.

"It's got to be after noon already. Let's call Lawson," Cat said.

We walked into the kitchen, where Cat arranged the video like before, showing just her face, with the same blank wall behind her. She connected, and Lawson's voice said "Leave a message." She looked over at me, as if to ask me what to do next. I nodded encouragement.

"Crab night Tuesday," she said. "We'll call back. Um, you should try Mom at six tonight." Cat then quickly disconnected.

"What if he thinks it's a trap or something? The guy is really paranoid," Becca said.

"I didn't want to say too much to a recording. If he's not there to answer the phone, maybe the muscle guys have him, or are listening in. Or both. Shit," Cat said. "What do we do now?"

"We try again in an hour. In the meantime, I'll call Sam to set up the dumpster inspection, and Jacob to see if he knows anything about Lawson," I said.

I set the camera back to wide angle, and called Sam. He was in his office, motioning someone to leave the room. "Hey J.T.," he said, pausing at the sight of the two women. He looked about to say something, and then reconsidered. "You have something?"

"We emptied the trash outside the lab," I said. "We found Margaret Jackson's DNA on some paper cups and plastic spoons. But we don't know if she's still there. But tomorrow, the trash goes into an empty dumpster. If Stanley's acting abilities hold up, he should be able to get fresh samples. I can send you the chip codes for her and you can compare."

"And what am I going to tell a judge to get a warrant for that?" Sam asked.

"Nothing. It's out in the open. But if you need to get retentive on it, you can always get a warrant and come back for another sample. I'm sure by then we can generate some probable cause." I tried not to smile. That never works with Sam.

"Don't fuck things up, asshole. I'll get Johnson to look in the trash." Sam looked annoyed. But he always looked annoyed.

"Also, we're kind of counting on the regular squad car visits at six to scare away the goblins," I said. "Can you let me know if there are any plans to change that?"

"You are not going in there," Sam said.

"Not us. Jerry Lawson," I said.

"And why wouldn't I just pull Lawson in for a conversation as soon as we see him?" Sam asked.

"You haven't yet, and he comes around pretty regularly. I think you're using him, just like we are. I rather expect he's got a voice transponder in sleep mode on him somewhere, maybe in some change he got from a delivery boy. He is cash only these days, am I right?" I looked at Sam's image on the screen.

"For that I'd need a warrant," Sam said.

"I'm sure he's high on your material witness list," I said. "But no matter. Help us get him in. Tonight, if he starts answering his phone. Any idea why he might not be answering?"

"I couldn't tell you that," Sam said, "even if I knew. Protocols and procedures. You're not an official player here."

"Yes, sir, Captain, sir," I said, saluting. "I'll let you know when we find out."

"The very minute you find out," Sam said. "And stay away from Bayside, you hear?"

"And have you arrest me again? I'll bet they'd love that down at the station."

"Give it up, asshole," Sam said, and disconnected.

Cat looked at me carefully. "I'm getting to know you, Mr. Wright," she said. "You didn't actually promise not to go there."

"Just keeping options open," I said. "No plans are set in concrete, not just yet, anyway."

I called Jacob. "Hey, Jake," I said. "Sam's in on the trash removal plan. And I think he'll notify us if the schedule changes on the drive by. We can't reach Lawson, any ideas why?"

"He may be asleep. He's been driving all night. He spotted the police tail, and spent the night trying to lose them. Went halfway to Los Angeles. He's in a motel while his car recharges." The address of the motel showed up on the screen.

I looked over at Cat. "Then it's unlikely he'll be back by six tonight," I said.

"Not likely. But he did lose the tail. The cops should use UAVs like we did. By the way, you bought six of them, just so you know. They don't have a lot of air time on a charge, so we have to rotate them." Jacob seemed pleased with himself.

"They sound like fun toys," I said. "Maybe we can find something fun to do with them when this is all over."

"By the way, more goons arrived from down south. They're carrying a lot of ferrous metal. Sniffers are picking up gun oil. Either that or they carry around sewing machines. Something may be coming to a head." Jacob seemed to look from one of the women to the other.

"Let's just hope it doesn't happen until tomorrow night at six," I said.

"Jonathan Worthington's on the radar again. We couldn't tell what he was loading into the car, but he's been shopping at hardware stores and sports equipment places, and an automotive shop. Quite a bit of stuff, locked up in a big steamer trunk and a duffle bag. He had to buy a new car, more of a truck, a big sucker, four-wheel drive, big metal grill out front, makes him really easy to follow. I'd put low odds on him going camping on the weekend."

"Interesting. Was this before or after the reinforcements from October Nine came in? Are they aware of one another?" I asked.

"Can't tell. He's spotted the goons watching the lab. Don't know if they suspect him, he's been careful. But now he's going to stick out like a five-legged dog, driving that thing. Everyone's going to remember that rig driving around. The goons have been trickling in. No reason to think he's noticed more of them around."

"I'm not sure I like Worthington getting active," I said. "We've no reason to think he'll be predictable."

"One more thing," Jacob said. "We've got those tails on the consulate people. And the consulate guy we call "number five" has been sniffing around the goons, but we followed him to Lawson's place last night, too. Slippery guy, we lost him several times, only found him at Lawson's because we've got it staked out. Professional."

"You may want to keep your distance there. He'll show up at the places you're watching, or else he's not worth following. Let Sam know about him. Tell Sam you're leaving him to the pros."

"Will do. That's about all." Something beeped on his desk, and he looked up at a screen. "Oh," he said, looking back at the camera. "Sarah says to tell Becca it's tonight, at eight. I have no idea what she's talking about."

We all turned to Becca. She put on a "who, me?" face, and said "Well, I guess I have a date."

I looked back at Jacob, who shrugged. I disconnected.

"OK, spill," Cat said to Becca. "Every time I find you in a room by yourself, you're on the phone to someone, and every time you switch to some nature channel as soon as I come near. Who have you been putting on hold all those times?"

"It wasn't always Jimmy," Becca said. "Sometimes it's Susan, sometimes Sarah, sometimes Rosalind or Maria, once it was Grace."

"All of the women who have Jack on their shit list?" Cat asked.

"Not all of them. Just the ones I've met personally," Becca said defensively.

I held up my hand towards Cat. "You make it sound like a bad thing, that she's making new friends."

"She's being a snoop," Cat insisted.

"The beauty of having no secrets is that there's no such thing," I said. "Either of you can ask me anything you like, and I'll tell you. But some questions are hard to ask. Then you ask someone you feel more comfortable with. And that makes it easy to make new friends, having something in common to complain about."

Cat looked at Becca, and both of them burst out laughing.

"If you need a car tonight, just pick one," I said to Becca.

I started to call Sam back to tell him Lawson's address. Cat caught my eye first. "I'll be in the back room with my locket," she said. "I may be up really late — don't wait up for me." I nodded. Becca waved and headed off to the media room, probably to call one of her new friends, or to let Jimmy know she'd scored the limo for the evening.

Sam was still in his office. "Lawson is at this address," I said, sending the text to his screen.

"You talked to him?" Sam asked.

"No, Jake has better help than the city can afford. We're still arms length with Worthington. I did tip him off about the goons, though. No sense getting him killed by ignorance."

Sam had that "Sam" look on his face again. "Is that why he bought a 400-kilowatt off-road vehicle? Any idea what he's got in the box? Something I should know about?"

"Something he got at a hardware store, and a sporting goods place," I said.

"They sell guns at sporting goods stores," Sam said, pedantically. Never a good tone to use with me.

"Not without a waiting period," I said. "He hasn't been in California long enough for that."

Sam's face changed to a more thoughtful countenance. That had not occurred to him. He was apparently not getting enough sleep.

"Sporting goods, and a hardware store. Doesn't seem likely he bought a tent for a night in the woods after off-roading."

"That's what Jake thought too," I said. "Get some sleep, Sam, you look like you've been through the wash."

"Who sleeps these days? Oh, right, you do. They keeping you up at night? I hear rumors."

"You can learn a lot that way," I said. "Get some sleep. Things are coming to a head. You'll want to be sharp."

"Stay safe, J.T.," Sam said. "I mean that," and he disconnected.

I walked to the hallway. I could see light under the door in the room where Cat had secreted herself. I went upstairs to work for a while. Eventually, it got late, and I went to bed alone.

When I awoke, I was still alone. The screen on the wall was flashing for attention, stating that it was 3:24 in the morning. I had the house answer in voice-only mode. Sam's face showed on the screen.

"Thought I'd get put through to your machine," he said. I have the house set for privacy only when I'm alone. Sam knew that, and was surprised that I was alone. I made the phone go to full video.

"What have you got?" I asked.

"One of the O9s at the lab has turned up dead. Across the street, actually, where he usually watches the front door of the lab. We had a man on him, and he didn't see anything. Professionally done, real quiet. A taser and then an injection of potassium chloride in the carotid. The guy watching the back is still there, hasn't a clue his buddy clocked in. The body just came in a few minutes ago. The lab report just hit my desk. Massive dose, no attempt to hide the injection point."

"And you're thinking who?" I asked.

"Worthington's on the list," Sam said.

"Very unlikely. Jake will know if he's back in town yet, though. Although your man would hardly miss the new ride. But you used the word 'professionally', so you know it isn't Worthington. Are you keeping tabs on your friends from the embassy?"

"I thought your theory was that they liked exotic military nerve agents," Sam said.

"They may have been sending a message with that," I said. "Maybe this time it wasn't about sending messages. Something more pragmatic. Did anyone break into the lab? By the front door? If your people go near the lab, have them wear protection, don't touch anything. Have them tested for either of the binary components. For that matter, have the dead goon tested, too."

"I told you, he died of the injection," Sam said.

"You need to know if he's been exposed to one or the other of the components of the nerve agent," I said. "Roland Drake might not have been a message. He may have been a test run."

"Then why wouldn't they use it this time?" Sam said.

"It might not be a quiet way to go. Get some sleep, Sam. You're not on your game."

Sam gave me a sullen look. "I'll have him tested. I'll have Stan wipe down the front door and have that tested too. Using gloves."

"I'll send you something I cooked up," I said. "A nasal spray, good for about a week. If you suddenly smell cinnamon and roses at the same time, you're near one or the other of the components. Of course, if you're near enough to both to smell it, you're probably dead." I sent the data file with the recipe. Sam's lab could make some up in an hour or two. "Get some to Stan, and he won't have to swab. He'll be able to just sniff around."

"When did you cook this shit up?" Sam asked.

"It took a while," I said. "I did it the slow way. Recombinant yeast. Your guys will feed it into an ACT synthesizer. I never needed one of those, so I never bought one. Maybe I'll pick one up." I might need to. My yeast were still out in the greenhouse, and I had never checked on them, so I didn't actually know if they were still alive in the brew tank. The machinery was automatic, but had to be fed nutrients every once in a while.

Sam waved at the camera and disconnected. The room was dark again. I went back to sleep.

§

Chapter Nineteen

Cat was in the bed when I awoke. The sun was up, and I got out of bed quietly, and walked downstairs without bothering to get dressed. The grass on the way to the greenhouse was cold and wet on my bare feet. The hot shower felt good.

In the lab, the yeast were brewing fine. The automated machinery had been doing its job. I poured some of the culture into a drinking glass and added some QuikLyze to break up the cell walls, and then centrifuged the mixture. The result was a clear amber fluid above the sediment, and I didn't bother to refine it further. As a nasal spray, it would work fine as it was. Having no sprayer, I improvised with a pipette. It stung a bit in my nose, but it would do. I filled two more pipettes, and took them and the centrifuge vial into the house, and quietly went back into the bedroom to get dressed. Cat turned in the bed, but did not wake up, or at least chose to return to sleep.

I went in to the study to call the police. I was hoping Sam was sleeping, so I called the front desk and asked for Stanley Johnson. He looked like he had not had much sleep either.

"Long time no see," he said warily. "To what do I owe the honor?"

"I'm working with Sam on the October Nine thing," I said. "Did you get the nasal spray yet?"

Johnson looked suspicious. "I'm not at liberty to talk about police business with taxpayers," he said.

"Then you did. Excellent. I assume with all of last night's excitement you haven't yet had a chance to get the evidence from the dumpster. But I'm sending the DNA barcodes Sam wanted to compare it to. They should come up on your screen in a few seconds. We're expecting a match on at least one of the food containers or spoons or something, to tell us your material witness was in there yesterday."

"That's what all the trash collecting was about?" Johnson asked.

"Oh, you got it already? That's great! Good thing I caught you, so you can send the barcodes to the lab right away. Sam's been running ragged. He'll really appreciate the help. Did you get a chance to test the nasal spray in the morgue?"

"The morgue?"

"I guess not. Check it out, you'll like this one. Instead of formaldehyde and death, the place should smell like roses and cinnamon. You probably won't even have to go in the door. You'll probably get the same smell anytime you're near one of the October Nine guys. Like an early warning signal."

Johnson sniffed the air, an uncertain look on his face. "I'll check that out. You're sure it's the morgue and not the gym?"

"You smelled it in the gym?" I asked.

"Yeah, cinnamon and flowers, like some guy wearing too much cheap cologne."

"In the police gym," I said, thoughtfully. "Keep that to yourself and Sam for the moment. Anybody smelling like that to you, be very careful what you say to them about this business, you hear? That smell is your secret weapon, it can tell you who to trust and who not to trust. Anyone coming up smelling like a rose is someone to watch, as long as you are also smelling cinnamon at the same time," I said, keeping a quiet conspiratorial voice.

"They got someone in the department?" Johnson asked.

"Smells like it, from what you say," I said. "But listen — if something smells like that, don't touch it. The spray lets you smell the components of the toxin used on Roland Drake. You don't want to end up like the guy who collected Drake's hat."

Johnson nodded, eyes narrowing a little in thought. I jumped in before he could say anything. "If you go down to the morgue, you should smell it — coming from the dead goon from last night. Do that, and if Sam is around, let him know it works. If Sam isn't around, call me at this number, and let me know if it worked or not, so I can fix any problems. And let Sam know right away if the test on the trash comes up positive, or call me if Sam's not in yet. That will save us a lot of time."

"Gotcha," he said, nodding. I disconnected before his brain could engage, and realize that a civilian was giving him orders.

Someone in the police gym had been exposed. Had they gotten contaminated by touching the dead body? Or were they also being targeted for extinction? Or was the delivery method sloppy, painting more targets than it should? Things began to fall into place in the back of my head, where all the coincidence detectors hid.

I called Jacob.

"Hi Jack. One of the goons turned up dead last night, you hear about that yet?" he said, getting right to business.

"Sam called me. Taser followed by a large injection of potassium chloride. Did your guys see anything?" I asked.

"The guy liked to hang around in the shadows. It was quiet, nobody saw a thing until our infrared camera noticed he was getting cold. We phoned it in, and the locals took over."

"Was there anything useful on the IR video replay?" I asked, knowing the answer.

"Negatory. The guy knew where the cameras were. He stayed behind the goon, or behind the wall all the time. The guy's a pro. My bet's on 'number five'," Jacob said.

"I said as much to Sam last night. How's our boy down south doing?"

"Lawson's on his way back. No sign of a tail yet, but he's taking some weird side trips just in case. He'll be a while getting here. You still doing calls at noon? He should be local by then."

"Yeah," I said, "We'll be giving him the call. How are the goons taking the news, by the way?"

"They're in pairs now, like they should have been all along. Makes them easier to keep track of, so that's one good thing. They're probably trigger happy now, I mean more so than before."

"I talked to Stanley Johnson. He's been given the nasal spray I talked to you about, I sent the recipe to Sam so the lab guys could play with it. He says he smelled cinnamon and roses on some guy in the police gym."

Jacob thought about that for a while. "Could be O9 has someone on the inside that has been painted. Or it could be a painter. Hell, it could be one of the cops who brought the dead guy in. That's most likely, but boring. Does Sam know this yet?"

"He will, Stan thinks he's James Bond now, and the bad guys are around every corner. Which is good. He'll keep his eyes open, and report any little thing."

Jacob looked into the camera for a moment, deciding whether to ask his next question. "So, what was eight o'clock all about?"

"If Becca wants me to know, I'll know in a few minutes. She played it as a date with James Dupree. But Sarah made the call, as soon as someone in your office let her know you were talking to me. Sarah loves games, I suspect Susan is in on it, and James Dupree was never in the picture. Sarah wants you and me to know about it, and wonder about it. It involves one of us. My bet is you."

"Just what I need right now, another distraction. I'm not going to play Sarah's games. I'm just going to let them hit me with whatever it is, whenever they do."

I smiled. "I'll send you something in a plain brown box. Don't open it until Susan wins the game."

Jacob gave me a puzzled look. I responded. "Sarah's game involves me somehow. I can play without getting distracted."

He shook his head slowly, and reached up to disconnect.

Downstairs, Becca was making omelets again, using whatever she found in the refrigerator that had color. I considered skipping breakfast, but she was finishing the third one when I walked in. Someone was going to have to teach her to cook.

"Cat down yet?" she asked.

"She was up until the wee hours. I tried not to wake her."

She looked down at the plate with the omelet in it. "How do I keep this warm until she comes down?"

"Tell the oven to keep the plate warm," I said. The oven behind her lit up as it heard me, and she turned around to put the plate inside.

"You have the weirdest house I've ever been in," she said.

"The voice recognition in the house is perfectly normal. I just have all the appliances connected to the main house net," I said, a little defensively.

"Everybody else just has knobs on things. It's a lot simpler that way."

"I live alone. I need someone to talk to," I said, smiling.

She looked at me for a moment, her eyes focused on mine. "You should fix that."

She carried the plates over to the table, which had been set somewhat randomly. I sat down and took a bite, ready to wash it down quickly with a gulp of orange juice. But the omelet was actually rather good.

I told Becca the details of last night and this morning.

"We're still on for six tonight, right?" she asked. "Having twice as many bad guys watching? They'll still go away when the cops drive around, right?"

"We'll have to make Lawson feel safe," I said. "But if we can, the plan is still to go in. Unless we hear she isn't there. We should know before noon. Stanley Johnson should have the barcode scan results pretty soon."

"You don't think she's there, do you? You think the reason all the bottles are thrown away unopened is that they just want us to think she's there. Do you think she's dead?"

"We'll know soon enough. Let's assume she's going to have a chat with us at six. But let's not walk into the building if we know she isn't there. Lawson seems to genuinely believe he can take us to her. He's nervous, but that's likely to be on account of the muscle knocking off his buddy."

Sam called as we were cleaning up our late breakfast.

"Stan says he had an interesting conversation with you this morning," he said.

I looked at Sam's face in the big screen. "How much sleep did you get this morning?"

"Enough. He says the morgue reeks of flowers and spice. And that the barcodes you sent him match the trash from the dumpster. Don't go around me, J.T., I don't like that. You need something from the police department, you ask me, or you go through normal channels, you get me?"

"Had your coffee yet, Sam? You're a little touchy. Johnson's a good guy. Now he's an alert good guy. But I have a question for you. What do October Nine goons and cops that use the gym have in common?"

"He mentioned that," Sam said.

"No, I mean, what else do they have in common? Someone's getting AC 13 catalyst into the goons somehow. What if it's in the performance enhancing drugs they take? And if some of those illegal drugs had been picked up by the police, who would have access to the evidence? Someone who might like the idea of performance enhancing drugs? I'm just saying, Stan can sniff around and tell you which of your people should not be anywhere near October Nine suspects when they might be targeted for elimination. Some spillover might cause collateral casualties."

Sam looked tired. "I'll have someone look into that. I don't have a lot of people I can throw in that direction, J.T., I have everybody out on the street watching for that other shoe to drop."

"You might want to take a snort of the juice yourself, Sam. Along with anyone staking out the lab or the goons. It could be important to know when AC 13 components are around."

"I'll take that under advisement," he said.

"Oh, Lawson should be back in town by noon or before. We're still counting on him being able to get inside at six. Let me know if something is about to gum that up."

"Nothing's changed, at least not yet. He can have a full police escort if he likes, I'd love to get someone in there for a look around," he said.

"I doubt he'd go for that. But if I need to, I'll mention it."

Sam waved at the camera, then disconnected.

Cat came down the stairs, hair in disarray, wearing one of my white T shirts and apparently nothing else. She yawned. "Smells like breakfast down here," she said. "Am I too late?"

"In the oven," Becca said. "If it's all dried up, blame Jack. He said to put it in there."

"Remind me to tell you about radishes," Cat said. "I couldn't go to bed until I finished that whole story."

I caught Cat up on the evening's activities, and the morning phone calls.

"Dead goon. That's good, right? One less testosterone fueled bigot killer in the neighborhood? And some ninja super spy looking out for our welfare?" Cat said, yawning again.

"I doubt we're part of the plan for either of them," I said. "Hopefully, they aren't even aware of us. Sam still has your father as a suspect in this latest. Taser and needle — he could do that. But Jacob found no rhinovirus at the scene. Still, Sam might have to take him in."

"Where's Dad now?" Becca asked.

"We're deliberately not tailing him," I said. "What we don't know, we can deny knowing in court. The virus lets us pick up the trail pretty quickly if we need to, but even that should be petering out by now. But he's driving a big four-wheel drive car that's easy to recognize, so I don't think anyone will have any trouble finding him. If he's in the city, under directed traffic, Sam can just call the ITC and find out where the car is at any time. If he's driving manually somewhere outside the city, he's both safe and not a problem."

Cat poured a thick layer of ketchup all over the omelet and began eating. Becca seemed not to be bothered by the condiment smothering of her creation. I called Jacob.

"It's almost noon," I said. "Do we know where Lawson is?"

"He's at home. He circled the block about six times. I think he has all the neighbors' license plates memorized. He never looked up, though, so he didn't spot our flying toys. But no goons are watching the house, and Sam's people are off somewhere else as well."

"Just for curiosity, do we know where Jonathan Worthington is?" I asked.

"No, but we could find out if it's important," Jacob said. "He's in the city somewhere."

"No bother, just curiosity," I said. "We're on for tonight. Margaret Jackson is in the building, and the O9 in the morgue is positive for AC 13 catalyst. I suspect someone got it into their injectables. That's hard to do — it means they probably have someone in the supply chain."

"We'll have extra manpower at six, then, to make sure nothing goes wrong. I'd like to bring by some ear canal radios, so we can stay in touch. Only your doctor would know you're wearing them, but I'll be able to hear what you hear, and keep you aware of what's going on outside."

"Can we all get some?" Becca asked.

"I'll bring plenty," Jacob said. "I'll be by around two o'clock if that's OK."

"Sounds good," I said. "We're going to give Lawson a call, to see if he's up for it."

Jacob waited a second, then disconnected.

I went upstairs to make a private call. Cat was still eating, and Becca was unlikely to follow, so I would have a few minutes to play Sarah's game. I called Grace at Etienne's.

"Do you remember the dress Susan Baker wore to the party last week? The red low cut with the ruby? I'd like to get her something like it, but a little less risqué, something really special though. Something good for a party at an embassy, as opposed to the Academy Awards."

"I'm sure I can hunt something up," she said. "How much time do I have?"

"Is tomorrow evening too soon?" I asked.

"You men," she said. "But sometimes I do my best work under pressure."

"Gift wrap it, and then put that into a plain brown box, and deliver it to Jacob Bennington. I'll send the address in a second by text."

"Is this to be a surprise?" Grace asked, rhetorically.

"Absolutely. I am counting on your famous discretion." I winked, and disconnected after sending the address.

It was exactly noon when I came back down to the kitchen. Cat had brushed her hair back with her fingers, and was sitting in her usual place for the phone call. Since the camera would be focused on her face, it didn't matter that the T shirt was almost see-through. I sat down next to Becca, and Cat made the call.

"Crab night Wednesday," she said. "Or Tuesday if you didn't get our message yesterday."

"I got the message. I was indisposed," came the low quiet voice.

"There's a police car that tours the biotech park at Bayside at six every evening. The tattoos are noticeably scarce at that time. We can walk in without being bothered," Cat said, trying to match the cloak and dagger atmosphere.

"How long are they gone?" Lawson asked.

"Twenty minutes minimum," Cat said, making up a number. I nodded encouragement to her.

"I'd rather enter without police supervision. We'll follow the police car from a good distance, and get out at the door. I'll send the car home without us. Be prepared to spend the night."

"We can do that. There will be three of us," Cat said.

"The big guy who was at the door with you?" Lawson asked.

"Yes. He's a friend."

"No weapons, or you won't get in the door," Lawson said.

"No weapons. He's more the deadly sarcasm type anyway," Cat said, looking over at me.

"There's a convenience store at the corner of Tulare and Palm. Meet me there at twenty to six, in the parking lot." He disconnected without waiting for a reply.

I looked at Cat and Becca. "There's something I'd like you to do to prepare for tonight. I cooked up a special trick in the greenhouse, something that will let your nose detect either of the two components of the AC 13 nerve agent. Before we go into the Lawson's lab, I'd like all of us to be able to smell the toxin, so we know what to stay away from. I've already dosed myself, but I'll do it again to show you how."

In the greenhouse, I held up one of the pipettes. The amber fluid flowed down to the tip of the pipette, and I let a drop form there. Blocking one nostril, I held the drop up to the other, and inhaled quickly. The drop disappeared, and the slight sting made my eyes water.

"It stings just a little bit," I said. "But not a lot."

Becca looked dubious, but Cat reached for the pipette. She held it up to her nose, hesitated, then sniffed hard. She held her breath for a moment, then let it out, and blinked a few times. She sniffed.

"I don't smell anything different," she said. "Except maybe bread or beer."

"Good," I said. "I should hope there are no AC 13 components in the house."

Becca repeated Cat's performance, and then sneezed.

"Try that again," I said, "Just to be sure. There is no harmful dose."

Becca did it again, but without the sneeze this time. "This has got to be the weirdest vacation we've ever had," she said, looking over at Cat.

When two o'clock rolled around, Jacob found us by the pool, drying slowly in the sun. The house had let him in and directed him to us. He had a plastic case with him, which he opened on the glass table.

"These are the comm units I mentioned," he said, picking up a small beige twig out of the foam packaging. "They fit right into the ear canal, up where they can't be seen. You can still hear just fine, and they transmit about a hundred meters or so, and the batteries will last about nine hours."

He handed one to me, and watched as I fit it into my right ear. He pulled out a handset from the foam packing and turned it on. I heard a voice say "Ready" in my right ear. He then whispered into the handset.

"You're lucky they wore suits," I said, answering the whisper.

Cat and Becca put their earpieces in, and I could now hear them speak through the device, as well as through my normal hearing.

"You will all be able to hear each other speaking, even from as far as a hundred meters away," Jacob said. "You can also hear some of the background noise from the other earpieces, but it should be very low volume."

Cat and Becca immediately tested this feature, walking in opposite directions, counting off as if preparing for a duel. "This is totally James Bond," Becca said.

"That would make Jacob be 'Q', right?" Cat said.

"I've been called worse," Jacob said into the handset.

"Now you can whisper sweet nothings in his ear, and I won't miss a thing," Becca said.

I walked with Jacob back into the house while the women played around outside.

"This is the AC 13 detector," I said, holding up the centrifuge cartridge. "Just the supernatant, not the precipitate," I said. "You can put it into a nasal sprayer, or you can just snort a drop from the pipette like the three of us did."

"Smells like beer," Becca said. "Feels like snorting beer, too." Her voice came into my right ear, and also out of the speaker in the handset Jacob had put into his shirt pocket.

"In the presence of either component, you will get a simultaneous odor of cinnamon and roses. That means you're close to one or the other of the components. If you're close enough to both components to smell it, you're probably dead." I held the pipette to my nose, blocked a nostril, and pantomimed sniffing. I handed the pipette to Jacob. He looked a little doubtful, but sniffed up the drop quickly.

"Yeah," he said, blinking, "Like snorting beer."

"Do I have to take this thing out to swim?" came Becca's voice in my ear.

"Don't go too deep," Jacob said. "They can get wet, you can shower and bathe, but never dive deep with something in your ear."

There followed a splash, then another, and the women tried speaking underwater. It was not intelligible, except for the giggling.

"Go soak your head," I said, and more giggling commenced.

Throughout the afternoon the two played with their new toys. Their favorite activity became chewing on celery and potato chips, and belching. Jacob stayed until five o'clock, then left to oversee the preparations for the evening's activities. Cat had him count as he left, and the signal stopped at forty-six.

We changed out of our bathing suits, and I watched the clock. I had a feeling in my chest like I had just made an important move in chess, and I was waiting to see if my opponent noticed and countered. Cat and Becca were abnormally quiet. We picked the non-descript sedan, and had it drive us to the corner of Tulare and Palm. None of us spoke during the trip.

When we arrived, a voice in my right ear said "He's in the dark blue coupe." Cat and Becca immediately looked towards the car.

"We should probably be careful not to give away that we're hearing voices," I said.

Our car parked, and we walked over to Lawson's car. He indicated we were to get in with a silent jerk of his head. As soon as we were in the car, it started moving.

Cat began to speak. "So-" but was immediately interrupted as Lawson's hand shot up, palm open. He brought his finger to his lips. Cat nodded conspiratorially.

The car parked on the side of the road near the entrance to the Bayside biotech park. We were several minutes early, and we waited in silence. When the police car arrived on schedule, Lawson waited until it had turned the corner and was out of sight, then followed slowly.

We all scanned left and right, looking for signs we were being watched. There were a few parked cars in the lots, but no pedestrians visible. We stopped at the side of the building near the door. Lawson got out quickly, then hurried to the door. The three of us followed. By the time we caught up, he had coded in, and the biometric scanners had recognized him. He waited for us, and then quickly opened the door and slipped in.

We followed him into a small empty room, with another door and keypad opposite the one we had entered.

"Wait here while you are scanned," Lawson said.

A voice in my ear spoke up. "We're getting a terahertz spike out here. Looks like a weapons check."

Lawson spoke to the door. "Gerald Lawson and three guests to see Margaret Jackson." He turned to Cat, and indicated that she should speak to the door. "Catrina Worthington," she said.

Becca was next. "Rebecca Worthington."

"Jack Wright," I said when it was my turn. We waited for over a minute, but then the door clicked loudly. Lawson entered a code on the keypad, and swung the door open.

"I'm assuming that was a second locked door," Jacob's voice said in my ear. I walked in through the door into an open office space. "Let me know if you-" His voice cut out as the door swung shut behind us. Apparently, the building was shielded. This explained why Lawson hadn't just phoned in. Becca looked up at me, and Cat did as well, then jerked her head forward.

"Have you been having problems with your customers?" I asked Lawson.

"The athletes? They don't know we exist. All the customer contact is done in Romania." He seemed much more at ease now that we were inside the protection of the building and in familiar surroundings.

We were halfway into the large room when a door opened off to the side, and a woman walked in, followed by three men.

"Mom!" Becca called out, then ran towards the woman. Cat followed quickly, and they all hugged. The men looked awkward for a moment, and then joined Lawson and me.

"There's a police cruiser every night at six o'clock," Lawson said to one of the men. "The gangsters hide when it comes around, so we can get in and out without being followed."

I turned to Margaret Jackson. "Are you alright?" I asked. She seemed sober, well groomed, and her clothes showed no signs of having been slept in recently. She looked at me critically. "Who are you?" she asked.

"He's our friend," Cat said quickly. "Mom, meet Jack Wright. Jack, meet Mom. Jack's here to help."

One of the men looked up at me. "Doctor Jack Wright? Of Xenocor?"

"You're thinking of my brother Sam," I said. "I haven't been associated with Xenocor for a number of years now."

"You wrote the book on epigenetics, the blue helix book. I taught from that book at Berkeley," the man said, offering his hand. "George Kerlington," he said. "I've been running the lab here, since Doctor Rosing was killed."

I gave him a blank look. "Doctor Rosing started this place, almost thirty years ago. They followed him from Romania to Libya and shot him in broad daylight."

"They being the October Nine group?" I asked.

"The gangsters, big muscled jerks with tattoos. They followed the athletes to Romania to find out where they got the treatments. They tried to muscle in on the Romanian end of the business, but those guys wouldn't deal. The ones who aren't dead are hiding out. Then they followed Rosing, shot him, and took his briefcase. That's how they found this place."

Cat spoke up, looking at her mother. "We got your message, and came out here to find you. We were outside the store when the clerk got shot."

Margaret Jackson looked at the ground. "Tommy didn't know anything. I never thought he'd get killed."

I looked over at her. "What's your part in all of this?"

She looked up at me, then back at Cat and Becca. "I came back to find out what Jon had done to Catrina," she said. "All the secret work he couldn't talk about, then running away to Fort Detrick when I was three months pregnant with Catrina, then the arguments when I became pregnant with Rebecca. I knew he had done something in the lab when the IVF screening was done. I came back and after a few months I found James Rosing, and followed him."

"We didn't know anything about that," Kerlington said. "That all happened before any of us got here. I first met Maggie when Jason started bringing her around, before all the shit came down, before we had to start being careful about who came in the door."

"I followed everybody," she said. "For years. I found out where everyone lived, where they spent their time when they weren't working. I picked Jason because he went to AA and to the liquor store. He seemed," she paused, "he seemed like someone I could manipulate easily. I got a job at the store, and started going to the meetings. We became drinking buddies. Eventually, he told me what they do here, making genes for the athletes. Genes that can't be detected. Selling them in secret to people in eastern Europe."

"We got scared when Doctor Rosing was killed," Kerlington said. "It was time to quit. But we knew they'd find us and make us stay in business if we just gave up, so we came up with the plan. We get a sample out to the press, and blow the whole thing sky high. We would call the FBI and get immunity, and then go public. Once it was public, the athletes couldn't use it anymore, and the gangsters would leave us alone, because we'd have nothing they could use."

"And then Jason gave the sample to Maggie, to hide in the freezer at the store. Then he got the idea to tell the gangsters they could have thirty percent if they let us alone, or nothing if we quit and went public. He said he had the sample on ice, and if they didn't go for the deal, it went straight to the press."

Lawson broke in. "That really pissed them off. They took Jason and kept him somewhere for four days. Then they killed him and dumped the body. He'd been tortured for four days. But he didn't tell them where the sample was. It took them weeks to figure it out. In the mean time, they played like they were accepting the deal. They wanted half the profits, but the guys in Romania had gone into hiding, so there wasn't anything getting sold. They started advertizing. They let the word out that they had some secret genetic lab that could do all kinds of things."

Margaret looked at Cat and Becca. "Someone broke into my apartment and tore the place up. I hid out on the roof of the stationery store, but they went to the liquor store and shot Tommy. When I heard about that, I came here. They can't get in here. This place is like a fortress. If they tried to break in, everyone in the park would notice. But we got stuck here. Every time we went out, we'd see them waiting."

I looked over at Kerlington. "Do you know who killed Roland Drake?"

"Who is Roland Drake?" he said.

"The gangster that shot Tommy at the liquor store," I said. "He was killed shortly afterwards, and the sample was taken from him. You had no part in that?"

"Kill one of those guys? Are you nuts? They'd tear us to pieces. And I'm sure the FBI wouldn't cut any deals if we killed someone. We're in enough trouble as it is. Do you know how many Olympic records will be tossed out when this comes to light? We're hoping for witness protection," Kerlington said.

"Perhaps a customer of yours might be killing off gangsters? Another one was taken out last night, just across the street from here," I said.

"The athletes? They don't know we're here. They think this stuff comes from Chechnya or something," Lawson said.

I looked at Margaret Jackson. "How about Jonathan Worthington?"

She lifted her head. "I expect he's here by now. God knows I left enough breadcrumbs. All he has to do is look at the joint bank card statements to see a fifth of Southern Comfort delivered here every day. He'll know what to do. He's the smartest person I've ever known. Much smarter than that Rosing idiot. Jon knew when to get out. He just stayed long enough to make sure Cat didn't have Hinshaw Barnes."

"Well, actually Mom, he stayed a little bit longer than that. But that's a story for another time. What do you think Dad is going to do?" Cat said.

"I don't know. I'd have to be as smart as him. But he'll figure it all out. Honey, if I'd known people were going to get killed, I would never have sent you that message. You'd be safe in Maryland. Away from all this."

As she finished speaking, the building rocked as if in an earthquake, and a loud crash could be heard from somewhere in the back.

"The lab!" Kerlington shouted. "Who's in the lab?"

Lawson looked around. "We're all here. No one is back there. What could blow up back there? It's just a wet lab."

In my right ear a voice was coming in and out, breaking up. "...around the...check to see..."

"How do we get to the lab?" I asked Kerlington. He started running towards another keypad protected steel door. I ran after him, Cat at my heels. He got the door open, and the voice in my ear came in loud and clear.

"...and make sure he's not injured," came Jacob's voice.

"Jake," I said, "What's going on outside? We're all fine in here, for the moment."

"Worthington backed his truck into the building, at about ninety miles an hour. There's a big hole in the wall, and we can't see the truck at all. But there are at least a dozen goons running towards the building, maybe more. I have my people holding back for the moment. The goons are heavily armed, they just went into the hole in the wall after the truck. I've called Sam's people in. They'll be here any minute."

"Becca," I said, knowing she could hear me even though she was still in the other room. Get everyone into a safe place. Lawson will know where. I'm going to find Jonathan."

"Me too," Cat said. Kerlington had not heard about the October Nine incursion, and was keeping up with Cat and me as we hurried down a hallway towards the noise. "Your gangsters are coming in," I said to him. "You might want to find a place to hide."

He looked at me, thinking. "Where are you going?"

"Jonathan Worthington crashed his truck through the wall. That's how they're getting in. I'm going to find out if he's all right."

"You'll need me. I know my way around, and I have the door codes," he said.

We stopped at the end of the hallway and listened for sounds of motion around the corner. "If you were Jonathan Worthington, and you wanted to crash through a wall and then do as much damage as possible, where would you be right now?"

"The machine room. All the computers are there, and the freezers. Take those out, then this place is out of business for good. That's by design. No offsite backups. Everything can be flushed of evidence in a hurry if the police raid the place."

"That's where he'll be. Jacob, where is the hole in the wall?"

"Southwest corner, south facing."

"He crashed into the south wall, near the west end of the building. What's there?" I asked Kerlington.

"The old loading docks. The big doors were framed in and stuccoed. Anywhere else and he'd have hit solid concrete. It's a tilt-slab building."

"How do we get to the machine room?" I asked.

He pointed around the corner. I checked, and that hallway was clear. I started down it, Cat and Kerlington close behind. It ended at a door with a keypad.

"Number five just went in after the goons," came Jacob's voice in my ear.

"Great," I said, "just what we need, another unpredictable variable."

"Sam's here too. Where are you?" Jacob said.

"We're heading for the machine room, Worthington's likely target. East side of the building, near the center. Sam's best bet is to just knock down the doors with the keypads. They're just framed in with wood. There are three doors so far, we'll prop this one open. He can knock down the front door, and the door on the south wall once he gets in, on the right. Then he can just follow the doors that are propped open to get to us."

"Got that, J.T.," came Sam's voice. "SWAT's here, piece of cake."

"Becca, are you close to the front door? Maybe Lawson can open it, save some time," I said.

"No, we're way back in the snack room. We pushed the fridge over against the door," Becca's voice came back.

"Stay put then. Wait for the police," I said.

Kerlington had opened the door, and I wedged a pen into the door-frame to keep it open. We could hear the crash of the SWAT team opening the front door. We went down the hallway and were about to turn another corner when Cat grabbed my arm, her finger over her lips. She sniffed. I smelled it too, a distinct odor of roses and cinnamon. We waited for sounds of footsteps, but heard nothing.

Crouching low, I quickly put my head out into the hallway and pulled back again. There was a can in the hallway, emitting a weak hissing sound. I stood up, then turned the corner. Cat and Kerlington followed.

"Don't touch anything," I said. "We won't be able to tell which has the catalyst and which has the gas. The gas is harmless without the catalyst, but the catalyst could be anywhere."

We turned the next corner and found two of the heavily tattooed and muscled gangsters lying in the hallway. "Especially don't touch *them*," I said. We stepped over the bodies carefully. There was an-other loud bang behind us as the second door was battered down.

The door ahead of us had been opened using the simple technique of knocking off the keypad and doorknob with a sledge hammer. The door was half open. Peeking around it, I saw a tall thin man wearing a backpack, and holding a can like the one we had found in the hallway. He pulled at the top, and the can began hissing. He tossed the can into the room.

Behind him, I could see what had to be Jonathan Worthington, his back to us, pouring liquid from a metal can into a large freezer.

The thin man raised a gun and aimed at Worthington. "Stop what you are doing and step away from the machine," he said, in a voice with an accent that reminded me more of Singapore than China.

Worthington set the can down slowly, on its side, so the liquid con-tinued to spill out. He held something behind him as he turned to face the man we knew only as number five.

"I'd like to thank you," he said slowly, "for taking care of my family."

At first, I thought he was talking to me, but it seemed unlikely he could see us in the dark hallway. There was a shot from behind him, and the freezer burst into flames. The flare gun he had hidden behind his back was now visible in his right hand. Worthington raised the flare gun to point at the thin man, but the man shot first, hitting Worthington in the chest, first once, then two more times. He walked over to him, and pointed the weapon at Worthington's head.

Before he could pull the trigger, there was a tremendous explosion near my left ear. Sam's pistol shot hit the thin man in the back of the head, and the far wall became dark with the remains of the man's face.

"Daddy!" Cat screamed, and ran towards Worthington. Sam and I ran after her, followed by half the SWAT team.

The fire was burning extremely hot, and had spread quickly to the other pools of liquid under the computers and lab equipment. The SWAT team pulled the two bodies out of the fire and back down the corridor where we had entered. Automatic sprinklers were spraying water everywhere except the machine room, where Worthington had disabled the inert gas fire system. As water washed into the room from connecting hallways, it spread the flaming liquid throughout the room.

Sam and Cat were rushing after the SWAT team. I stayed behind, assessing the damage to the room, the heat hitting my face painfully. I picked up the gun the thin man had dropped, and aimed at the remaining cans of acetone and paint thinner. Three shots later, the fire was fiercely burning the computers and the memory storage cabinets. I tossed the gun into the blazing freezer, and ran down the corridor after Sam and Cat, closing the steel door behind me.

Leaping over the bodies of the two October Nine intruders, I caught up with Sam, who was breathing heavily. Cat and the SWAT team were ahead of us, running through the battered door into the main office space. I kept pace with Sam as we followed the others through the office and out the front door.

I stood and caught my breath, and took in the scene.

Becca and the knot of lab employees were standing on the lawn, talking with Wilson, the criminal lawyer Jacob had brought in. I imagined the conversation being rather one-sided, composed mostly of warnings not to say anything to anyone. Jacob saw Sam and me come out of the building, and ran towards us.

"The hazmat team is on the way to clear out the O9 bodies. We counted fourteen altogether. Two died outside after getting a whiff of gas from the building. The fire department is here, but they aren't allowed inside until the hazmat team gives the OK. They're hosing down the roof, but that part of the building is going to be nothing but powder and ash in a few minutes."

Worthington and the thin man were already in bags, awaiting the hazmat team's inspection. Cat was sitting by her father's body, weeping softly. When Wilson was done with the group from the snack room, Becca and Margaret Jackson joined her. I left them there, and motioned to Jacob to follow me over to Wilson. Together, we gathered Kerlington and Lawson and the other GenePharm employees and took them out of earshot of the others.

"The main bulk of the October Nine movement is dead," I said. "I suspect the remainder are not long for this world. The lab is completely destroyed, including all biological samples and all computer records of what was going on there. No one connected to the sale of undetectable genetic performance enhancers knows where they originated, except for those who are dead. The only people who know how to make them are here. And no one knows that you possess that knowledge."

They all stayed silent, looking at me intently. "An agent of a foreign government, using banned chemical weapons, has taken out a group of people dedicated to the extinction of non-white people. I suspect that aspect of this whole mess will quietly disappear. At this point, there appears to be no evidence connecting any of you to any illegal activity. You had some proprietary technology which was sought after by a group that no longer exists. That technology and the knowledge of how to reproduce it was lost in the fire. What you require, at this point in your careers, are references from your former employer. Kerlington can provide that for everyone but himself. And I suspect Kerlington has already arranged for his future, is that correct?"

Kerlington nodded. I continued. "It appears, as Margaret Jackson predicted, that Jonathan Worthington has solved all your problems neatly. If you hold by your confidentiality agreements, I would expect no further trouble. Now you'll have to excuse me, as I have pressing business elsewhere."

The hazmat team had inspected the bodies of Worthington and the thin man, and Sam was arranging for the Worthingtons to be taken to the police station. The hazmat crew had moved on to the bodies of the October Nine members, and a special truck was being loaded with the bagged bodies. I walked up to stand next to Sam.

"You know I told you several times to stay away from this place," he said.

"I promised I'd take them to their mother," I said.

"So that Catrina could watch her father get murdered?" Sam did not approve.

"I assume that is how your report will read," I said. "He was murdered, and you shot the killer as he was preparing the coup de grâce?"

"You have a different view of what happened?" Sam asked.

"I think that's how the report should read. Clearly Worthington was murdered. Shot three times in the chest, and would have been shot again, probably in the head, if you hadn't intervened. I just want to make sure that an insurance policy that surely has a suicide clause is not subject to any misinterpretation. The underwriters of that policy no doubt expected Worthington to die of Hinshaw Barnes, for which he was not insured."

"Clearly, the man was murdered," Sam said. "It's really hard to shoot yourself in the chest three times from ten feet away. And this clearly wasn't suicide by cop, as the cop shot the other guy."

"Then I expect the family is about to come into a substantial amount of money," I said. "Margaret Jackson described her ex-husband as the smartest person she knew. I am coming to agree with her."

Sam stayed at the scene. I called my car, and had it drive me to the police station where the Worthingtons were. I found them talking to a desk sergeant. Cat saw me, and ran to me and buried her face in my chest. We hugged for a while, then she raised her face to look at me. "He did that on purpose. I heard what he said."

"He did that for you, and for himself. When you give your statement, describe only what you saw. Don't speculate. He didn't say 'children', he said 'family', and I suspect your mother could use some help from his insurance company."

She looked at me blankly for a moment. "He loved her, didn't he," she said, not making it a question.

"I think he loved you all," I said.

I was a long night. It was well into the dark part of the next day when the four of us arrived at the house. Becca showed her mother the room next to hers, and promised a full tour in the morning. Cat and I went upstairs, showered, and went to bed. It took Cat a long time to get to sleep. I watched over her until her breathing slowed, and then finally drifted off myself.

§

Chapter Twenty

Clay Garret was the first to arrive in the morning. I wasn't expecting visitors, but apparently Becca had been working the phones the previous night and in the morning. Clay brought Rosalind Bennet with him, and Margaret Jackson began telling stories about how she and Jonathan had met, and other happier days.

I was making the second pot of coffee when Sam arrived. "Mandatory suspension after any shooting," he said. "Came by to see how everyone was doing."

"I'm just fine," I said. "But I didn't just shoot someone. How are you?"

"Do it again in a second," he said. "Just wish I'd done it half a minute earlier."

"Jonathan Worthington would disagree. He had planned his final minutes pretty carefully," I said, waving to the kitchen table. "They know it, they just need some time to get used to it."

When Jacob showed up with Susan, it was time to call in some help. I called Sarah Collins and had her arrange for a catered lunch, and had her invite anyone that Becca had made a connection with in the past two weeks, and anyone from Jacob's team who had helped in the search for Maggie. Clay Garret seemed to approve. The larger the support group the better.

By lunchtime, the group was indeed large, and had moved mostly out by the pool. Jacob, Sam and I were sitting at a table in the shade of one of my father's big apple trees. Holding a beer, Jacob puzzled over one question. "Why were the bottles of Southern Comfort tossed out unopened?"

Sam answered. "She can't drink anymore. She'd been taking disulfuram and naltrexone pills on and off for years, but when she moved into the lab, she had another option. They could give her a shot that would keep her body from converting acetaldehyde into acetic acid. Permanently, unlike the pills. So now when she drinks, it's unpleasant to nauseating, instant hangover. The gene is patented, but those guys never bothered with royalty payments, or prescriptions, or doctors."

"Better than the Manheim protocol," Becca said, joining our table. Cat, Clay, and Maggie joined us with her. "Cat says you should tell us about radishes", Becca said.

Sam looked at Becca and said, "I think juvenile records are sealed," he said.

"Actually, I'd like to hear how Sam tells the story," I said. "Besides, half the people in the swimming pool already know it, as well as Clay here."

"He's just trying to ruin my image as a professional in the department," Sam said. "Because it all started when Dad caught me smoking marijuana. I was, what, eleven at the time? John Thomas was maybe eight. I caught hell, because the new psychedelic strain was illegal. Probably still is, but nobody cares anymore. J.T. started reading about the drug, to see what Dad was so upset about. He found out that some guy in the Netherlands had published the sequences for the whole pathwway that produced tetrahydrocannabinol, the active ingredient. "

Sam paused to take a breath. "At school they were growing radishes, because they're so easy for kids to grow, and they grow really fast. It turns out that radishes are closely related to a little weed called Arabidopsis, which is probably the most researched plant in the world, one of the first to be fully sequenced. So, he goes into the greenhouse and adds the pathway to a radish. But he doesn't just add one copy. He puts in 22 copies of the gene, and makes sure that all of them are expressed. Three weeks later, he has a crop of radishes, and another couple of weeks he has a bunch of seeds."

Jacob began to shake his head and smile. Sam continued. "He sends a bunch of the seeds to the guy in Holland, and a bunch to a local medical marijuana growing group, and who knows where else. The radishes have so much THC in the leaves and flowers and roots that you get totally wasted just chewing on a leaf."

Jacob broke in. "But so far he hadn't actually done anything illegal, had he?"

"No," Sam answered, "at least, nothing ever went to court, so we'll never know. But in six months time, you could find the radishes anywhere you went in the whole world. Whole industries in California, Mexico, Turkey, the Philippines, all over the world crashed, and some places had serious local recessions. Crime rates in border areas dropped by half. And without major drug cartels pushing it, marijuana just went away. But since the radish was legal and everywhere, it didn't have the attractiveness of a forbidden illegal drug, and people just moved on to other things, mostly designer drugs."

"So," Jacob said, "an eight-year-old took down some of the largest drug cartels in the world, and eliminated whole industries, with a school science project."

"Actually," I said, "it was just a garden. They weren't teaching science with them, just showing how plants grow."

Cat looked at Clay Garret. "It's a good thing Sam told the story. When Jack tells it, it takes forever."

Clay agreed. "He is somewhat detail oriented."

I turned to Cat. "So, what are your plans now? I mean as a family," I said, waving at Maggie and Becca.

Maggie spoke. "Well, first we bury Jon. His folks have a plot for him up in Napa where he grew up. Then we will probably want to sell the house in Maryland, since the girls seem hell-bent on moving to California to finish their education. Split three ways, that should give me enough for a down on a little place, and put the girls through school."

"Split two ways, Mom," said Cat. "I came into a substantial sum a little while ago, that will keep me in school for as long as I want."

"And," I said, "I don't see her paying a lot of rent in the future, if I get my way." Cat kicked me under the table, but she was grinning widely. "I also think you should check Jon's insurance policies before making any long-term plans. You may have more money than you think."

"Maria says I should stay with her at Windcall and change my major to architecture at Santa Cruz," Becca said. "She says nobody makes a lot of money as an art major."

"Money isn't everything, honey," Maggie said.

"Oh, I plan to make lots of money," Becca said. "I love spending money."

About this book

The germs for many of the ideas in this book come from meetings I've had over the last five years with some truly extraordinary minds and people.

The ideas for genetic approaches to longer lifespans came from three discussions with Doctor Aubrey David Nicholas Jasper de Grey, two of them when I worked at Google and he came to give talks, and one later after I had left Google to run my own companies, and we were both invited to the third SciFoo scientific conference.

It was at the second SciFoo conference that I met Doctor Steven Benner, and I have since had the pleasure of two discussions over lunch with the man who created the field of synthetic biology. Our discussions ranged over dozens of topics on which he had deep knowledge, and small molecule therapeutics, bioinformatics, and protein sequence databases made it into this book, and I am sure his work in evolutionary bioinformatics, and paleomolecular biology will make it into subsequent novels someday.

It was also through talks at Google and the SciFoo meetings that I had the opportunity for long talks with Doctor Hugh Rienhoff, the clinical geneticist who has spent the last four years studying his daughter's DNA to find out what particular changes led to her unique genetic makeup. An entrepreneur, physician, corporate Chairman and CEO, this amazing man talked about buying used sequencing equipment on eBay to do the work at home.

But it was meeting Greg Bear and Neal Stephenson at the SciFoo conferences that led to much of the flavor of this book. Neal described his task as "putting the 'hard' back in hard science fiction", and that thought resonated as I wrote this book, treading a fine line between the needs of the story and the characters, and the duty to stay close to the real science whenever possible.

My friends and former co-workers at Google have not yet invented inference searching, and when they do, it will no doubt be faster than I have made it appear in this work. But the knowledge I gained in almost five years of working with the brightest minds in web search have brought some amount of insight, I hope, into what computers may be doing in the next 100 years.

Lastly, some of the recipes and food ideas in the book came from discussions with my friend Elise Bauer, who runs the popular web site Simply Recipes. She is in no way responsible for any of the atrocious things Cat and Becca came up with, except in the sense that one day we were discussing horrible things to do to food, such as putting mustard on ice cream, I let slip that I occasionally smothered omelets with ketchup, which she found somewhat shameful.

I invite the reader to Google all of these names, as these are people you will definitely want to know more about.

Simon Quellen Field, November 2008

About the Author

My name is Simon Quellen Field. When I am not writing novels, I write books about science and computers, and I run the company Kinetic MicroScience, LLC, and the web site scitoys.com.

I live on a 20-acre farm in the Santa Cruz mountains, overlooking Silicon Valley, where we raise chickens, goats, alpacas, parrots, bearded dragons and other assorted creatures, in addition to a small vineyard and a growing assortment of fruit trees.